The Tree Elves of Ludlow

The Tree Elves of Ludlow

Archie Hunter

The Book Guild Ltd

First published in Great Britain in 2023 by
The Book Guild Ltd
Unit E2 Airfield Business Park,
Harrison Road, Market Harborough,
Leicestershire. LE16 7UL
Tel: 0116 2792299
www.bookguild.co.uk
Email: info@bookguild.co.uk
Twitter: @bookguild

Typeset in 12pt Minion Pro

Printed on FSC accredited paper
Printed and bound in Great Britain by 4edge Limited

ISBN 978 1915603 708

British Library Cataloguing in Publication Data.
A catalogue record for this book is available from the British Library.

For all the real people in this book.
My wife Milly, my children; Archie, William & Henry,
my step children; Lexi, Tom & Flora.

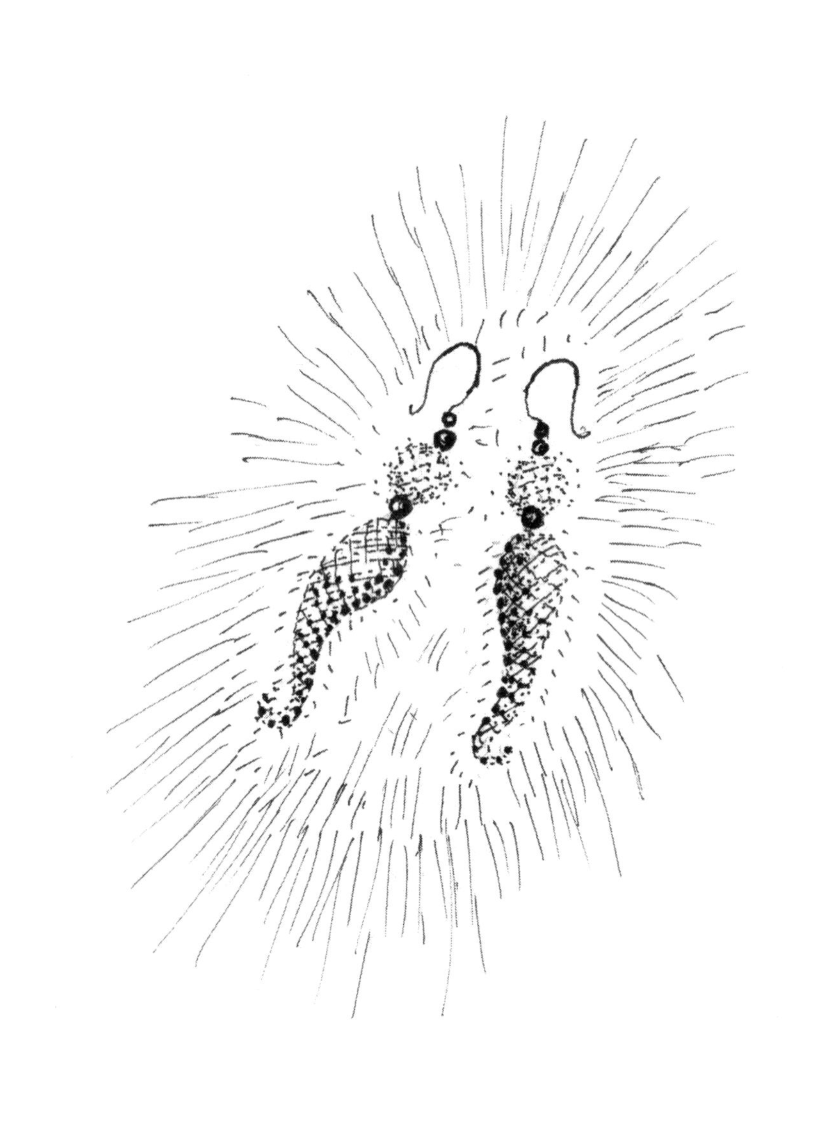

Prologue

If you have ever smelled the smell of a goblin, you will never ever forget it as long as you live.

It's not just repugnant. The oily, rotten stench claws at the back of your throat, creeps into your hair and stains your clothes. But that is not all: the smell is evil, menacing and, above all else, it creates fear.

These memories flashed uncomfortably through Henry's mind as he held the car at a steady and purposeful pace in the direction of Ludlow. Despite the comfort and security of the car, these familiar thoughts sent an involuntary shiver down his spine.

It wasn't long before the car was climbing, dipping and twisting through Mortimer Forest. The tall pines along the road threw pillars of deep shadow across the path of the car, making it flicker in and out of the sunlight. After reaching the highest point in the forest, the car began its gentle run down towards the Teme river valley and the town of Ludlow.

During the descent, the woodland lifted to give a window on the Shropshire countryside and through a lattice of trees there were snatches of Ludlow Castle and the town spilling out at its feet. Now close to the bottom of the hill, the car slowed in anticipation of a turning and, without indicating, pulled off the road onto a lay-by that was both a lovers' rendezvous and a popular picnic spot.

For a time the car was motionless, parked in silence as if it was digesting its journey. Eventually the driver's door opened and Henry emerged with the help of a walking stick. With care, he made for a green bench but chose not to sit down. Standing behind the bench, he leant heavily on the backrest with one hand and with the other shielded his eyes to gaze over the town below.

On the air came all the noises of a drowsy town on a warm summer's evening: the purr of traffic, children's laughter, lazy dogs barking and the half-hour chime of St Laurence's Church clock. But this was no ordinary town. What stood it apart was not the orange glow that now bounced off its Georgian streets or the authority of its castle. Nor was it the small and graceful river that circled round to the south of the town. Few towns in England can match these qualities, but they were not the reasons why the old man stared out from the bench.

It was the old calling that stole up from out of the fabric of Ludlow, washing into every corner of his body.

It slipped effortlessly into his mind, making him tingle from his head to his toes. He was no stranger to these feelings and he absorbed them without apprehension.

Henry also knew that this was the last time; it was his goodbye. But before he could close the door on all that had happened to him there was still one more duty required of him.

Back in the car, the old man rejoined the road and headed off down towards the town. Before crossing Ludford Bridge, the car swung left into the car park behind the Charlton Arms Hotel. Watching over centuries of travellers, the hotel still stands sentinel over the bridge and offers hospitality to weary feet. But this time the sweet smell of beer and tobacco was ignored, and Henry hobbled past and onto the bridge.

Crossing the road to look downriver, he leant once more for support against the parapet. In one movement his right hand slipped in and out of his pocket and for a moment he held his clenched fist out in front of him. Glancing back at the river he laid his palm open to reveal a tiny musical instrument. The flute was no longer than the width of his hand and the casual observer would have been forgiven if they felt it warranted little interest because of its size. But a more careful inspection would have shown something quite different. The miniature flute was made of ivory covered with a painstakingly carved scene of an enchanted valley. In the centre of the landscape was a herd of wild goats, each with a bell, grazing on the sloping sides of the valley. Below the tiny mouthpiece was a band of silver on which was an inscription. The antiquated words were not of any contemporary language, its message lost and meaningless to any modern eye. It was clear the flute was not made for any human hands to play; it was crafted for nimble, delicate fingers that belonged to another world.

Henry rubbed his thumb momentarily over the silver words as if to provide comfort and reassurance, then flung back his arm and threw the flute out over the river as hard as a fielder throws a cricket ball at the stumps. His eyes followed closely the last moments of the flute until it hit the water with a tiny splash and vanished.

He waited, holding his breath for some acknowledgement of his deed. Such was the magnitude of his action he would have liked a sign… no, he needed a sign that recognised his part of an agreement made many years ago. But there was nothing. No thunderclaps, no rushing winds or eagle soaring over his head. The river was hushed and the sun was casting its final shadows. So the old man turned and reluctantly started his walk back to the car.

This time the public bar was too much to resist. There were a few people inside, but he wanted just his own company. He ordered a drink and retreated to a corner with a view overlooking the Teme. The beer was excellent and it started to reverse his melancholy mood of moments ago on the bridge. Henry watched as the last teal crumpled from the sky to the reed beds below. Across the river the townspeople settled down for the night, their riverside houses spreading a shimmering checkerboard of lights across the black water.

As he stared out of the window, there opposite him on a shingle bank protruding into the river was a lone figure. Its face and dress were indistinguishable in the fading light, but the familiarity of the figure meant he would have recognised it whatever the time of day. As he watched, the figure bowed and then was gone.

Despite his age and resolve, big wet tears built up in his eyes. Of course he was grateful that his action had been acknowledged, but it was the emotional mix of relief and regrets that momentarily overwhelmed him.

The old man, now feeling more snug and secure, briefly closed his eyes and in an instant he was back in his bedroom on the morning it had all began, so many years ago.

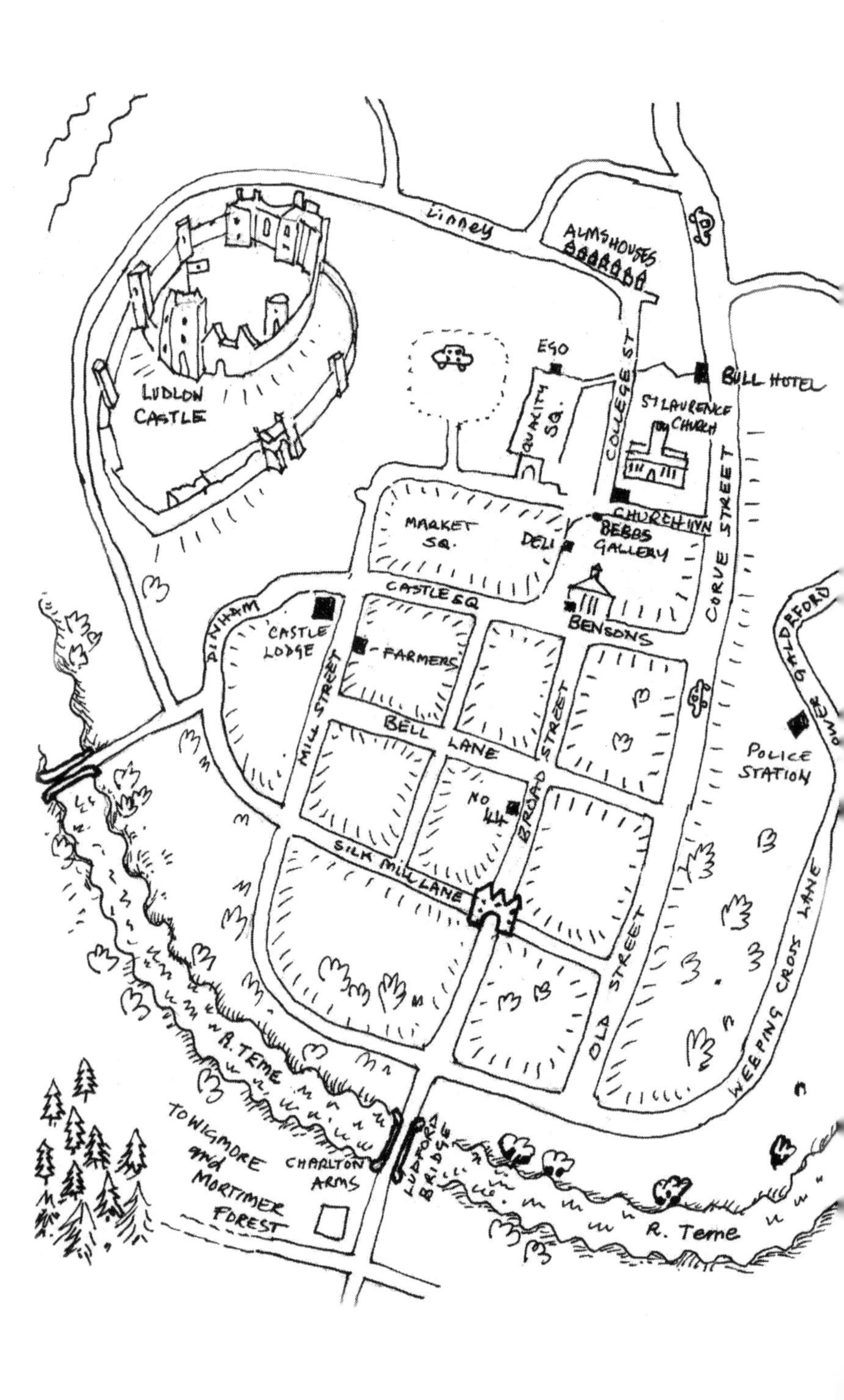

Linney
ALMSHOUSES
LUDLOW CASTLE
EGO
QUALITY SQ.
COLLEGE ST
BULL HOTEL
ST LAURENCE CHURCH
CHURCH INN
MARKET SQ.
DELI
BEBBS GALLERY
CORVE STREET
CASTLE SQ
DINHAM
CASTLE LODGE
FARMERS
BENSONS
GALDEFORD
LOWER
MILL STREET
BELL LANE
BROAD STREET
POLICE STATION
NO 44
SILK MILL LANE
OLD STREET
WEEPING CROSS LANE
R. Teme
TOWIGMORE and MORTIMER FOREST
CHARLTON ARMS
LUDFORD BRIDGE
R. Teme

Chapter 1

Henry shot his left leg out from under the duvet and then quickly retrieved it. This was a morning ritual that he played, teasing his foot with the chilly air of his bedroom and then rewarding it by returning it to the warmth of the bed. The game could never last very long and the result was always the same. He had to get up. It was no different that morning and, throwing off the duvet, he was through the door to the bathroom before the cold got to him.

In any case, today was worth getting up for. It was the morning of his first job. Even as he dressed, he felt a twinge of butterflies although, like all new starts, he was excited. Not so much about the job but about the money he'd earn! It was also the Ludlow Arts and Craft Fair in the castle grounds. The town would be full of people and by the evening there would be a few parties around the pubs.

After all the excitement of leaving school, finding a job had been tedious. There was nothing he could get animated about despite endlessly trawling the classifieds and registering with several job centres. In truth, Henry's lack of success was really down to one thing. His passion for racing. The chances of getting a proper job had been considerably reduced when his best friend's mother got him a weekend job at the stables at Downton Hall. Tom, who also worked at the stables, had started Henry's interest a few years ago whilst they were at school together, and now they both lived and breathed the racing world.

Tom, always an optimist, had said, 'You'd be mad not to take this job. It's just the break people dream about. Once you get the hang of things and they see how keen you are, well, all sorts of doors could open for you.'

'I know you are right,' said Henry with some caution in his voice, 'but what about going to Australia? I'm not going to earn an airfare in six months.'

Anyway, he had gone ahead regardless and loved every minute of his time at the stables. But the problem of earning some hard cash still hovered over him.

Tom's family lived in Ludlow and his mother had generously suggested that Henry could use one of their spare rooms for the summer. He would be nearer to Downton and, with his ear closer to the ground, he might find work in the town. Besides, Tom's mother, Milly, was something of a Mrs Fixit; she knew everything and everybody in Ludlow. Under her wing he was sure a job would walk through the door.

Curiously, the job at Bensons, the jewellers and clock repairers by the Butter Cross, found him rather than the other way round. He had gone to Bensons to get a new watch strap and whilst checking the selection had spotted a 'wanted notice' for a part-time assistant. Suddenly it seemed ideal. He had always had a bit of an interest in clocks and at the back of his mind he thought he might learn a thing or two about their mechanism.

Mr Benson was the only other person in the shop. He was a small, round, courteous man who always wore the same neat cardigan with leather buttons and a tartan woollen tie. His gold-rimmed glasses were balanced on his forehead. Every time he examined a piece of jewellery or a watch, he would bring his glasses to his nose in an accentuated flourish to show off his expertise. To be fair, Mr Benson was very good. He had been in business for over thirty years and there was nothing that his little jewellery shop couldn't offer. To his loyal customers in the town his work was quick, reliable and didn't cost the earth.

Henry decided on a watch strap and, as he handed over his money, he cleared his throat and asked, 'Could you tell me about the job?'

Mr Benson showed no surprise and quickly took in the young man in front of him.

'Well,' he said slowly, 'I need a person to come in the mornings or afternoons, to help me out with general things around the shop.'

Mid-sentence he decided he liked the young man in front of him and with a half-smile continued, 'It's five pounds an hour, starting nine sharp till one o'clock. Afternoons… I'd say one to five thirty.' As an afterthought he added, 'If you were any good… I might teach you a bit of what I know.'

Rather to his own surprise Henry heard himself saying yes to the job. After the to-be-expected schoolmasterish pep talk about dress standards and punctuality, they shook hands and Henry agreed to start on the following Saturday.

Now it was Saturday and his plans that day had been carefully organised. Contemplating the day ahead as he came down the stairs, his mind turned over what lay in wait for him. After he had finished at Bensons in the morning, he would race back home, quickly change and then it was up to Downton till six. Then the plan was to meet up with Tom and others back in Ludlow for the Arts and Crafts Fair in the castle. Then, smiling to himself, after that anything could happen.

As Henry was getting up and dressing for his big day, the situation across the landing from his bedroom couldn't have been more different. Flora, Tom's sister, was still in bed and she had every intention of staying there as long as possible. Her long blonde hair was scattered across the pillow and the duvet was half hanging off the bed. The rest of the room was in equal disarray, with clothes and shoes strewn across the floor.

Long after Henry had left the house, Flora's mother peered round her bedroom door.

'If you want to go to the Arts and Craft Fair this morning,' said her mother, 'you had better get a move on as we are going to Shrewsbury this afternoon.' Flora's reputation for morning grumps was renowned, so her mother ignored the sharp 'leave me alone' and went back downstairs to the kitchen. Fortunately her morning blues were short lived and before long Flora appeared at the kitchen door.

'Mum, next weekend what am I going to wear?' asked Flora as she slumped down at the kitchen table.

'I have no idea what you are talking about.'

'Tara's party!' said Flora, exasperated that her mother wasn't quicker off the mark.

'Oh that! Well, for heaven's sake, you've got a mass of clothes, try picking some off the floor, you never know what you might find,' replied her mother, laughing as she disappeared with an armful of washing.

After a cup of tea and a yoghurt, Flora grabbed her things, shouted a goodbye and headed out of the house to the Arts and Crafts Fair. On her way she called Tara, hoping that she could meet her and they could wander around the various stands together. But there was no response from her house or her mobile. *That's annoying*, thought Flora. But they would be a bit rushed if she had to get back for the trip to Shrewsbury.

Chapter 2

Flora headed up Broad Street and then turned left towards the Market Square. It was nearly eleven o'clock and already the square was full of people either busying themselves in the market or making their way towards the castle and the fair. Flora loved the market, and rather than skirt round by the pavement, she walked through the middle of the stalls looking left and right, always on the lookout for something that would interest her. Emerging from the cover of the stalls at the far end of the square, she was not surprised to see a huge queue of people waiting patiently to buy their tickets at the castle gate.

As Flora approached the entrance, she reached into her bag for the pass her mother had put in her hand just as she left the house. She smiled to herself as she waved the green card at the security man. Her mother always seemed to get free passes to everything; how did she do it? Flora weaved quickly in and out of the queuing people as they shuffled through the entrance lanes. She didn't have time to get stuck in a crowd. Leaving the shadow of the gatehouse, she walked into bright sunshine, but before taking a further step she paused to look up at the castle and the scene in front of her.

Her eyes ran over the familiar ramparts, the towers and thick stone walls that loomed over the fair. The castle, dating back to Norman times, had been an important medieval stronghold at the heart of the Welsh Marches. Its formidable position had for centuries protected the town from marauding armies. She remembered reading about how the kings of England made regular use of Ludlow Castle, fighting bloody battles with the Welsh and later bringing the intrigues of London court life to Ludlow.

The history lessons about the castle's illustrious and bloody past had stuck in Flora's mind. But what she really enjoyed most of all was pretending that she could travel back in time to experience living in a medieval town. Standing on the edge of the castle's outer bailey it was particularly easy to imagine the same fair six hundred years ago. For a second she closed her eyes, hearing a man shouting to fair-goers to guess the weight of his pig, the blacksmith's hammer on his anvil as he carried out a demonstration, and children's laughter. Nothing had changed. Even the smells would have been nearly the same. The air was scented with burning charcoal from the blacksmith's forge, there was a strong hint of ale from the beer tents and then the wind carried to her the sweet smell of a hog roast. She could have stood, watched and listened for longer, but time was ticking by and she needed at least an hour to have a good look at all the stalls.

Flora crossed the outer bailey to the first of the two large marquees. Inside the air was already stuffy from the mass of people circulating around the stalls. She wrinkled her nose at the prospect of mingling with so many people, but the stalls beckoned and she quickly became absorbed in her browsing. Stalls were arranged around the walls of the marquees, double-banked up the middle and selling everything under the sun: wood carvings, pictures, clothes, pottery and furniture too. Flora's favourites were the jewellery stalls. There was always a good choice ranging from modern to traditional, silver, tin or gold, necklaces, rings or bracelets. Everything a girl could want.

Last year Flora had found a particularly good jewellery stall so she was pleased when she spotted the same stall and recognised the owner. He was an oldish man with a tanned face and a neat pointy beard. He had several large earrings, one of which was a diamond stud. He wore a red and richly patterned kaftan, and when he stretched out his arms they were covered in bizarre-looking tattoos.

Flora would not have dared ask his name, but he seemed to recognise her.

‘How are you this year? I hope you haven’t lost that bracelet I sold you?’

Flora held out her left wrist to show a plain silver-coloured band. ‘Never take it off,’ she answered.

Fortunately somebody else came to the stall so she was able to start looking without being distracted any further. On the table in front of the stall was a collection of every kind of jewellery displayed in wooden compartments: rings in this one, necklaces in the next and earrings in another. Flora used her index finger to stir each compartment, hoping to see the perfect piece.

Then close to the bottom of the pile in the last box, she saw a pretty gold-coloured earring. It was a delicate but complex weave of fine metal strands set with a pattern of light blue stones. The strands came together at the top in a tiny sphere on which Flora could just make out some strange inscribed lettering. From the sphere there was a graceful metal hook.

Flora was entranced but was wily enough not to show it. Muttering under her breath but loud enough for the man to hear, ‘Pity there is only one of these,’ she said.

‘I’ve got the other one but it is missing the top bit,’ said the man without looking up, ‘but they’re special, that’s for sure.’ Flora turned the good earring over in the palm of her hand and waited. After a lengthy pause the stall owner broke the silence first. ‘OK, give me twenty pounds for the pair,’ dangling the other broken earring tantalisingly in front of Flora.

‘Twenty pounds! It will cost me that to have it repaired,’ said Flora in her best downbeat voice. She fell silent and looked directly at the man.

Another pause followed, only this time it was interrupted by another customer arriving at the stall. Not wishing to waste any more time, the man said, ‘Give me fifteen and it’s a deal.’

Flora would have liked to have worn the man down a bit more, but she really wanted the earrings. Besides, she was confident that she could sweet-talk Mr Benson into repairing them quickly and cheaply ready for Tara’s party next weekend.

She handed over her money and in return was given the earrings in a plain brown paper bag.

Chapter 3

Henry arrived at Bensons five minutes early.

'Good to see somebody is on time,' he heard a voice say behind him. Henry turned to see Mr Benson approaching and looking flustered. Searching for the shop key in his pocket, Mr Benson mumbled partly to himself and partly to Henry, 'Why does my sister always ring just as I am about to leave the house?'

'Marjorie is in bed with flu, so it is just you and me this morning,' said Mr Benson as he rattled the key in the lock and opened the door.

Between customers, Mr Benson went through all the routine matters relating to the running of the shop. First he showed Henry where different items of stock were kept: wristwatches in this cupboard, christening presents over here, clock repairs stored on these shelves. He showed Henry the big safe, but not the combination. Then he explained how to fill out a repair ticket, sales receipts and guarantees. Finally he gave a lesson on the use of the till and how to operate the credit card machine. When all was done, he gave Henry a test to check it had sunk in properly. Apart from a few minor mistakes, Henry passed comfortably and Mr Benson congratulated himself on his choice of new staff. Not only was he punctual but he was also quick off the mark.

Henry dealt with the next customer on his own and before long he was handling the expected rush of Saturday-morning customers without a second thought. Mr Benson beamed across the counter, getting happier by the minute with his new assistant.

The first sign of trouble that morning was unexpected and luckily there were no customers in the shop. Without any warning Mr Benson came out from behind his counter and as he moved towards the door he exploded, 'I'm fed up with this every Saturday,' and then disappeared outside. Henry rushed over to the window to see Mr Benson red in the face and waving his arms wildly. His irritation was all about a group of local boys gathered around a public bench that was a magnet for teenagers, particularly on a Saturday morning. There was a lot of laughter and shouting as several lads performed spectacular tricks with their bikes on the pavement just outside the shop.

The gang was made up of a mixed lot, but one boy, who clearly was the leader, stood out. His athletic figure was easily noticeable, as was his fair hair although that was partly coloured by red dye. He had a presence and the other boys obviously looked up to him. Henry recognised him. The other morning Tom had been reading the *Ludlow Journal* before breakfast and had read out to anybody listening that the same gang leader had been in court for fighting but had got off with a caution. 'Ridiculous,' Tom had said, holding up a mug shot. 'Why don't they lock him up?'

Henry watched with interest as Mr Benson singled out the leader. He couldn't hear exactly what Mr Benson was saying, but it must have had the desired effect. The boy shrugged his shoulders, turned and headed off in the direction of the market with the other gang members following close on his heels.

Mr Benson came back into the shop looking triumphant. 'That lot know they cannot push me about,' he said as he resumed his position behind the counter with an air of importance.

Henry was contemplating the incident, not sure that Mr Benson had really got the upper hand, when to his horror he saw Flora approaching the shop. 'What is she coming in here for?' he said out loud, without thinking. 'Typical,' he said to himself, 'just typical, I should have known that she would come in here to make me look stupid.'

The door chimed and in walked Flora. 'Morning, Mr Benson,' she said, then, 'Hi, Henry, sold anything yet?' in a singsong voice designed to cause him maximum embarrassment.

Mr Benson was old enough and wise enough to ignore the angled remarks and deliberately said, 'How can we help you, Flora?'

Flora produced her paper bag and emptied the contents onto the glass counter. 'I've just bought these earrings at the fair and one is missing the bit that goes into the ear,' she said. 'I am going to a party next weekend and really want to wear them.' Her voice trailed off as Mr Benson picked up the broken earring and screwed his magnifying eyepiece into his right eye.

There was silence as Mr Benson examined the broken earring. After a pause, he put down the earring and, without saying a word, picked up and studied the other one. Holding the good earring in the palm of his hand, he looked out of the window and up at the clouds scudding by. To those watching it was as if he was searching the sky for the answer to a question that was flying round his mind.

'I thought I knew it all,' he muttered, 'thought I knew it all,' his mind now apparently far away.

Flora jolted Mr Benson out of his trance. 'Mr Benson, I've got to go. Please can you let me know? Ring my mother. Henry knows the number,' she added with a giggle and was gone.

After Flora had left the shop, Mr Benson put the earrings in a small resealable plastic bag and labelled them with Flora's name and phone number, which Henry supplied. The earrings weren't put in the normal repairs box but in a drawer under the worktable in Mr

Benson's little workshop, just off to the side of the main shop.

Henry had known Mr Benson only for a morning, but anyone in his shoes would have noticed the change in the man after he had seen the earrings. He was talking to himself, shaking his head in puzzlement and then saying, 'Most interesting,' and, 'Very strange.' Henry wanted to ask him what all the excitement was about but thought better of it as Mr Benson no longer seemed in a talkative mood.

It was Mr Benson's habit on a Saturday morning to walk over to De Greys for a cup of coffee at about twelve noon. Today he was not going to make an exception even though it meant leaving an inexperienced assistant in charge of his shop. He needed to be on his own and he needed a strong cup of coffee.

'Henry, I have to go out for half an hour. You'll be alright, won't you?'

'No problem,' said Henry confidently.

As soon as the shop door closed Henry slipped round the counter and carefully watched Mr Benson cross the top of Broad Street and head towards De Grey's. Only after he had disappeared inside did Henry walk round to the workshop. Quickly settling himself into Mr Benson's old swivel chair, he pulled open the drawer and took out the bag containing the earrings. To the left of the worktop was an Anglepoise magnifying glass incorporating a lamp that Henry now switched on. Opening the plastic bag, he chose the good earring and pulled down the magnifying glass to get a better look.

Just at that moment the doorbell chimed and, cursing under his breath, Henry jumped up, for a moment thinking it might be Mr Benson returning earlier than expected. Fortunately it was only a customer wanting something repaired, which he quickly dealt with.

Back in the chair, Henry readjusted the magnifying glass and picked up the earring carefully. Up until now he had never shown the slightest bit of interest in jewellery and he certainly had no idea what he was looking at or looking for. With his eye to the magnifying glass, he slowly turned the earring over between his fingers. It was silky soft to touch and, as he moved it through his fingers, it flowed like molten metal. The fine weave of strands seemed to have no joins and the little blue stones seemed to float over the intricate twists of gold.

Henry jumped as his mobile rang. It was Tom. 'Hi, Henry, how is it going? I hear Flora came in to see you.' As Tom was talking, Henry quickly stuffed the earrings into their little bag, slipping them back into the drawer, and turned off the lamp behind the magnifying glass.

'Yes,' said Henry, 'would you believe it.' He paused. '…I hope it wasn't your idea?'

'Of course not,' said Tom, laughing. 'I'm on my way up, see you at one.'

‘Tom, do me a favour, in my room, on the chair is my rucksack.’ Henry was thinking fast. ‘Can you drop it off now? I need some stuff in it.’

A few minutes later Tom put his head round the shop door. ‘Here’s your rucksack; I’ll be back at one.’ Henry looked at his watch; it was nearly twelve thirty and Mr Benson would be back at any time.

Henry went back into the workshop, drew out the earrings and switched the lamp on again. Selecting the complete earring, he pushed his hand into his rucksack and pulled out his digital camera. He took a couple of quick close-up shots and then moved rapidly to put everything away.

It was past twelve thirty and no sign of Mr Benson. He was due to finish at one. Just then Tom tapped on the window and Henry waved to him to come in. ‘I’m on my own. Mr Benson’s not back yet,’ said Henry.

‘He’s just talking to somebody outside the shop. Looks like he is coming now,’ said Tom hopefully.

Mr Benson appeared at the door and his beaming face showed he had recovered to his normal self. ‘Well done, Henry, excellent first day,’ he said. ‘You’ve earned every penny this morning,’ clapping him on the back.

Chapter 4

The remainder of Saturday went exactly as planned. Henry and Tom arrived at the stables in good time to ride out and on their return the head lad put them to good use doing odd jobs around the yard. It was late afternoon before they got home. They made a quick turnaround then set off to join the mass of people beginning to enjoy a warm evening at the fair.

It wasn't until the early hours of the morning that they returned home and as they let themselves in Tom sighed. 'What a brilliant night. See you in the morning; thank goodness it's Sunday.'

'Mmm... it was great,' said Henry, but in truth he did not really mean it. All evening he was thinking about the earrings. And it annoyed him. He kept telling himself it was ridiculous to be mesmerised by something like earrings. But there was something, something that he couldn't put his finger on. He had seen Mr Benson thrown into confusion and, whilst he knew nothing about jewellery, it was obvious even to Henry that they were out of the ordinary.

Henry waited until Tom's bedroom door was closed, then fetched his camera from his bedroom. Back downstairs, he closed the door of the study and connected the camera to the computer. Once he had selected the best shot of the earring, he printed the picture, then closed down the computer and returned upstairs to his bedroom.

Just before turning his light off, he held the photograph close to his bedside light. He noticed for the first time the little sphere and the odd writing that covered its surface. Somehow he must have missed that when looking through the magnifying glass in the shop. Racking his brains, he couldn't recognise the writing and, as he turned off the light, unanswered questions were still racing around his head.

The following morning Henry woke late. Without anything on until evening stables, he decided to do a number of jobs that he had been putting off for too long.

One of the most pressing tasks was to plan his itinerary for his trip to Australia. Armed with a piece of toast and a cup of coffee he sat down in front of the computer and began putting together his schedule. It wasn't long, though, before his mind wandered off the subject, and he started to ponder what might be behind the strange events of yesterday.

Making sure that he was on his own, he opened the file containing the picture of the earring. He stared at the picture on the screen wondering. What was it that was so fascinating?

On the spur of the moment, he returned to the internet and did a quick search. His first search under 'earrings' produced far too many results. After several more false starts he typed in 'locally made jewellery in Shropshire'.

This time the results were more interesting. There were a number of jewellery makers in Shropshire. Henry had a look through their websites but nothing he saw came anywhere close to the quality or the intrigue of Flora's earrings. Scrolling down further through the search results, he kept his eye open for something different. He looked at several that listed special collections and exhibitions without success. He was rapidly losing interest when he spotted a website that specialised in 'Ancient jewellery, its history and mythology.'

He felt a surge of optimism, but as he scanned through the contents he realised they were too academic. Unconsciously, he clicked on the 'Contact Us' tab and was surprised to see that the author of the site lived in Shropshire.

The address was in Craven Arms, not far from Ludlow. He made a note of the details including the telephone number, feeling that at least it was a start. But it wasn't until a few days later that Henry acted on the information. He was coming down the stairs for breakfast and he could hear Tom's mother talking on the phone. When he heard the word 'earrings' several times, it became obvious that the call was from Mr Benson. Piecing together the conversation, Henry understood that the cost of mending them would be considerable. Mr Benson was trying to get Milly to sell the earrings rather than pay for the expensive repairs. But Tom's mother was adamant and said she would drop in later that morning and keep the earrings at home until she could afford the repairs.

When Henry came into the kitchen Milly looked upset.

'Morning, Henry,' she said, filling the kettle. 'I don't know what has got into Mr Benson, he seemed most strange just now on the telephone.'

'What did he want? It's a bit early… oh, was it for me?' said Henry, suddenly thinking that somehow Mr Benson might have found out about the photograph he took of the earrings.

'No, no, nothing to do with you,' she said, 'but… yes, it's funny that he rang so early. He sounds besotted by those earrings.' Now really talking to herself, she continued, 'Why would he want me to sell them? If they're that special, Flora should hang on to them… most odd.' Her voice trailed off as she put a cup of tea in front of Henry.

Henry ate a hasty breakfast as he was late for his lift

up to the stables. He could see the car waiting outside but still rushed up to his room and grabbed his pad on which he had written the contact details for the jewellery website.

Henry had a bad morning. Firstly they were late and the head lad gave him a lecture on wasting everyone's time if he couldn't get out of bed early enough. Then he fell off on the gallops. When he had got back to the yard and finished his other jobs, he was glad to accept a ride with a horsebox that could drop him off on the edge of Ludlow.

As he walked into the town centre he thought to himself that once again the earrings were having an effect on him. If he had been concentrating on his riding and not thinking about Mr Benson's call that morning, he would not have fallen off.

As he walked he felt the notepad in his pocket. Pulling it out, he reread the details. *Shall I or shan't I?* was going through his mind, but then without further hesitation he dialled the number on his mobile.

'Hello,' said a woman with a hard voice, 'Mrs Wergs.'

'Oh yes, hello,' said Henry, 'I wondered if you could help me? I saw your details online—'

Henry began to lose confidence, but Mrs Wergs interrupted, 'I can try.'

'Well,' continued Henry, who hadn't thought through this conversation, 'I am doing some research into local history and customs, and I had some questions about jewellery.'

‘Six o’clock tomorrow evening,’ said Mrs Wergs, sounding like she was giving an order rather than invitation. ‘After that I’m away for two weeks.’

‘OK, thank you,’ said Henry, but before he had finished, the phone had gone dead.

*

The following evening Henry caught the train from Ludlow to Craven Arms. Mrs Wergs lived at 37 Whitemeadow Crescent and the ticket office staff at the station pointed him in the right direction. It was a short walk and Henry turned into the crescent just a few minutes before six. The estate was about ten years old and was a mixture of detached and semi-detached houses built around a traditional village green. All were built of the same dark red brick and Henry was impressed with the overall neatness as he made his way round to number 37, a detached house in the far corner.

He knocked twice on the front door, as there was no doorbell. The door was opened almost immediately. Mrs Wergs was nothing like Henry had imagined. In his mind he expected an elderly lady, probably a grandmother with glasses and grey hair. But instead the woman stood in the doorframe was much younger with striking features. Mrs Wergs was in her early thirties, and about five foot tall. She had a neat figure but what distinguished her was her bird-like face and intense black hair that hung loose to her waist.

'Hi,' said Henry, 'I'm Henry, I rang yesterday... thanks for seeing me,' and he held out his hand to Mrs Wergs.

'Come in,' said Mrs Wergs, but she kept her hands to herself.

Henry followed her through the hall and into the sitting room. He was taken aback by the richness of the furniture and the decorations. There were Persian rugs, dull oil paintings in heavy frames on the walls and lace curtains that all but blocked out the light. On the mantelpiece was the ugliest of clocks that filled the room with its loud ticking. He was immediately reminded of Sherlock Holmes and almost expected to see gas lamps on the tables.

Mrs Wergs gave Henry a watery smile. 'Have a seat,' she said, pointing to a large and comfortable wing chair by the fireplace. She placed herself in an identical chair on the opposite side of the fire. 'Now tell me how I can help,' said Mrs Wergs without starting any small talk.

'Thanks for seeing me,' Henry started again with some awkwardness. 'I mentioned on the phone, I want to know a bit more about a piece of jewellery I think is quite old and it might have been made locally.'

'Have you got it with you?' chirped Mrs Wergs.

'No, I'm sorry,' replied Henry, 'but I have got a picture.' Henry took out of his jacket pocket the folded sheet of paper on which he had printed his photograph. He leant across the hearth and passed it to Mrs Wergs, who sat back and unfolded the paper.

The moment she looked at the picture it was as though the air was sucked from the room: the clock stopped ticking; even the flies on the window stopped buzzing. Henry's instinct was to run, to get out of the house as quickly as possible. But he was frozen, stuck to his chair, almost unable to breathe. Then worst of all, Mrs Wergs' appearance began to change. She seemed to age and wither into a bent, hunched old woman. Her skin tone seemed to change, her nose became hooked and her brow distorted. Henry saw her hands become long and bony, and her shiny hair was now lank and greasy. But Henry's heart turned to ice when he saw her eyes were now yellow.

Then in a flash Mrs Wergs looked quite normal. It was as if nothing had happened: the clock was ticking, the flies were buzzing and Henry shifted in his chair, checking that he could move.

She leant forward to give Henry the photograph back. The hardness had gone from her face and the mood in the room seemed quite different.

Henry, sensing the moment, said, 'The earring... do you know where it came from?'

'Yes, I do,' said Mrs Wergs. 'I have no doubts about it, but what I don't understand is why they have suddenly emerged after so long. Or why you have them? You do have both?'

‘Yes, I do, but where do they come from?’ Henry said with a hint of impatience.

It was as if Mrs Wergs couldn’t get the words out of her mouth. Then, with a real effort, she looked directly at Henry and said, ‘The earrings were made by elves.’

Chapter 5

Henry's laugh filled the room. It was the type of laugh someone makes when they've heard a good joke. 'Elves… you mean… fairy people?'

Another laugh escaped from him, this time more mocking, ridiculing Mrs Wergs' suggestion. He was about to say something witty until he became aware of her icy stare.

'If you want to know more about the earrings,' she snorted, 'you will have to listen to a history lesson.'

Henry kept silent. His mind was racing to work out the best way out of the house and onto the next train to Ludlow. After a pause Mrs Wergs got up. 'I think I'll put the kettle on.'

Unable to decide what to do, he watched Mrs Wergs disappear into the kitchen. His eyes roamed round the room, looking quizzically for anything out of place. But there seemed nothing out of the ordinary. He had already taken in the rich furnishings and now he noticed the usual family photographs and ornaments that decorate any normal sitting room. Still Henry felt uneasy; there was something missing but he couldn't put his finger on it.

Mrs Wergs reappeared with a tray with two cups of tea. It turned out she had already added the milk and there was no sugar on offer. She settled herself down again and, without asking Henry if he wanted to hear her out, launched into her promised history lesson.

'The events that I am going to describe took place during a period of history that is often forgotten about. Schools always start with the Romans and then jump straight to the Norman Conquest. There are about six hundred years between these two events.'

Oh no, thought Henry, *I don't need this.*

'During those six hundred years,' continued Mrs Wergs, 'England was a great wilderness. The country was one vast untamed forest. If you had climbed up the Long Mynd here in Shropshire, you would have seen nothing but mile upon mile of trees in every direction.

'You might think it idyllic: virgin forest, an abundance of game, wildflowers and clear, rushing streams. But for forest dwellers it was an isolated existence. Their life was hard, a hand-to-mouth existence. The men hunted and the women eked out an existence from the soil as well as bearing children. Winters were killers; lack of food, poor clothing… they were easy prey for the packs of wolves waiting in the trees. But it was not just wild animals that made for a short life.

'The country was divided into numerous kingdoms, most of whose names and rulers were never recorded. Kingdoms frequently changed hands as warlords constantly quarrelled and settled their differences with the sword. The real victims were, of course, the people and their meagre settlements, caught in the middle of somebody else's bloodbath. Burying your family and rebuilding your home was a regular experience for those poor peasants.

'No other region in the country typified this lawlessness more than Wales, particularly the Welsh Marches. The three dominant kingdoms, Gwynedd in the north, Dyfed in the south-west and Deheubarth in the south, were constantly at each other's throats. Have you heard of "Rhodri Mawr, The Great?" or "Merfyn Frych, The Freckled?" You would have... living in those days. Their names would have made your blood run cold.'

Mrs Wergs had a drink of her tea and continued.

'I am telling you all this because in the world that I've described there were actually two quite different people: the human world as you know it and the elfish kingdom of Gwydden.'

Henry glanced at the ugly clock on the mantelpiece. *This is getting worse*, he said to himself.

Keeping her eyes fixed on Henry's expressionless face, Mrs Wergs continued.

'Their ancient kingdom of Gwydden covered an area that stretched over most of Wales, into West Mercia and parts of the south-west. You might think it extraordinary that they co-existed with their human counterparts but never saw each other. This was possible only because of the elfish way of life. They too were woodland folk but past masters at the art of movement. Their use of light and shadow, and the sharpness of their eyes and ears, allowed them to slip unnoticed and silently around any clumsy human.

'Not only were they masters of the woods but they were also skilled craftsmen. And they had every reason to be. Because within their kingdom were the most priceless gold mines.'

Mrs Wergs let out a cackle of laughter, her eyes narrowing at the mention of the word gold. 'Yes... right under the noses of the humans. The mines were centuries old, deep in the Black Mountains. And the elves were clever with their gold and their works of art. They were thrifty folk. Wealth never went to their heads.

'Whilst anarchy existed in the human world, this was a time of peace for the elves. Their king, Cleddau, was a clever elf. Whilst he ruled with total authority he treated his people fairly, sharing his wealth, allowing his people to enjoy the good life. There was always plenty of music and good food in every elf's home. Elves are natural soldiers and King Cleddau built up an excellent army to protect his people and of course his gold mines. His people felt safe and they had little to worry about.

'Now King Cleddau had two sons who were total opposites. The eldest, Caled, was a bully, arrogant and lacking the handsome features of his father. The younger son, Grian, was a mirror image of his father, intelligent, charismatic and good-looking. As you might have guessed, the two brothers hated each other.

'It is the elfish practice, just as in some other cultures, for pre-arranged marriages. When the time came for Caled to marry, his father embarked on a search of his kingdom to find a suitable bride, hoping, of course, to find a woman who could help improve his son's character and in time make him worthy of the elfish crown.

'The search for a bride caused huge excitement across the land. Families with daughters talked late into the nights wondering, speculating and dreaming that their daughter would be chosen. They talked of the royal visitors, great feasts and their girls being called to the top table to meet the king and his son.

'But that was not this king's style. Instead he dressed as one of his subjects and, with only two of his favourite bodyguards, he passed unnoticed into the forest and began his quest. Over several months the undercover royal party worked its way methodically round the kingdom. Taking advantage of the natural hospitality of elves, they stayed with many different families, visited local hostelries and scores of busy markets.

'The story goes that the king and his party were lost deep in the forest and had to ask the way of a young girl tending her flock of geese. The men were tired and it started to rain, so she took them home to give them food and water. Their feet were in tatters from the miles they had covered so, after dressing their sores, the girl insisted that they stayed the night. It was only when she threw off her cloak that the king saw how lovely she was. Her name was Nior, which means perfect.

'Well, you can guess the rest… but you would be wrong.' Mrs Wergs sniggered.

Henry shifted in his chair; he couldn't pretend any longer that he wasn't interested in this strange tale.

'The king explained to Nior who he really was and why he was searching his kingdom. As you can imagine, both parents and daughter were plunged into a state of shock. But the king assured Nior that all her family would be well looked after and the days of scratching out a living in the forest were over. Without further delay the party started on its return journey. The group travelled in great secrecy and returned home without attracting any unwelcome attention.

'But soon the wedding was made public knowledge and preparations started for the occasion that would be the biggest celebration in most elves' lifetime. They came from all over the country for the spectacle, walking hundreds of miles to be witness to the special event. Elves of every age, shape and size. Nobody wanted to miss out.

'On the great day, in front of a huge crowd stood Caled with his father and his brother Grian, who by tradition was his best man. Both brothers were dressed in the ceremonial uniform of the king's bodyguard. You have to remember that nobody, save the king and his trusted bodyguards, had seen the bride. When she arrived the vast throng of people fell silent, but as she passed by in the flower-decked oxen cart there were gasps of awe at her elfin beauty.

'As she came closer to the royal party, the more important guests were able to have a closer look at their future queen. And once again there was an intake of breath as they took in her loveliness. It was not just her loveliness but what she was wearing. As a wedding present Caled had sent his bride a pair of earrings, the like of which had never been seen before.'

Henry felt the jolt of her words like an electric shock. For only the second time, Mrs Wergs smiled.

'They were no ordinary earrings. In the Black Mountains there was allegedly one elfin gold mine that was superior to all others. The gold that it produced was so pure, so beautiful and so sought after that its location was known to only a handful of the elves close to the king. I believe the mine was called Llyn Caigeann and to make the earrings the best craftsman in the kingdom worked for a month, hardly resting, using techniques unknown to any human, until his unique work of art was complete.

'The earring in your photograph is one of the

earrings he created for the bride on that extraordinary day.' Mrs Wergs finished with a triumphant look at Henry.

'Is that it?' said Henry. 'It doesn't really give me much to go on. You have told me a story, a legend, but it really won't help my research,' he continued, thinking he had the upper hand.

'No, it's not the end of the story,' said Mrs Wergs with more than a hint of menace in her voice.

'Nior approached the high platform on which the marriage was to be performed. In front of her were two men that she had never seen before, and one was to be her husband. As she climbed the steps she could see that the man on the left was scowling with heavy features and an air of aloofness. The other man was fair with striking features and was smiling down at her. Instinctively she thought this man was her future husband. In the final steps to the platform she rushed into the arms of Grian, hugging him in the excitement of the occasion. As one body, the huge crowd recoiled in shock as they witnessed the hideous mistake. Caled, who had a quick and violent temper, flew to the conclusion that his brother had orchestrated the situation as a deliberate slur on him. In the heat of the moment Caled drew his sword and Grian, seeing his brother's rage and thinking the young bride was in mortal danger, drew his sword too. The king's cries of anguish were drowned out as the two brothers clashed together.

'The two men were locked in each other's arms in mortal combat, then Grian slumped to the floor, fatally wounded. Nior watched in horror. The life of the man she thought was about to be her husband was slipping away in front of her eyes. In a desperate attempt to save him she threw herself down beside him. But in another cruel twist of fate, Grian believed his brother was about to strike again. In a feeble attempt of self-defence, he lifted his sword at the moment that Nior came to his help. Drawn in by her misplaced love and her unstoppable impetus, Grian's sword pierced her heart.

'The king fell to his knees to cradle his dead son. Then, mustering all his strength, he cursed Caled with the words, "Go below to live under the heel of your people until the end of the world."'

'How awful,' said Henry. 'That is terrible.' Then he checked himself, for he was beginning to believe this story, which was ridiculous.

'I am glad you were listening,' replied Mrs Wergs, 'but I haven't quite finished. The trauma of that day killed the old king as surely as if an arrow had gone through his heart too. The next day the elfish nation had to endure the pain of burying their beloved king, their favourite prince and the unfortunate Nior.

'Of course, in time the elves recovered, but they did not count on the resilience of Caled. As the curse said, he went underground and, with the few followers that went with him, he established his own kingdom and in time found a wife. Caled's people were known as the go-belows, but in time that got shortened to goblins.

'On Caled's deathbed he made his sons swear to continue to avenge his humiliation on his wedding day. Over the next two centuries the legacy of Caled guided the goblins to great victories over the elves. Without a strong king to lead them the elfish army was whittled away, and slowly but surely the goblin army took over the gold mines one by one.

'By now the goblins were a strong and independent nation. Their chieftain, a direct descendant of Caled, was a hard and intelligent goblin called Droch. The ultimate prize for Droch was the capture of Llyn Caigeann. Not only was it the wealth that tantalised him, but he knew that its capture would mean the end of the elfish people.

'The most important event in the calendar of elves was the Festival of Corran… The Festival of Arrows. Each year the best archers in the land gathered for a keenly contested match. The competition carried with it a carnival atmosphere, and there was plenty of music, drinking and dancing.

'This particular year, Droch's spies had been out watching the preparations for the festival. The information coming in couldn't have been better and his brilliant plan began to take shape.

'The festival got off to an excellent start. The crowd was a record size and the competition was fast and furious. By the evening the victor ludorum had been carried through cheering crowds and the party had started. And then the goblins attacked. The archers were exhausted from their competitions, their arms tired and sore from pulling their bows. And most of the arrows were still in the butts or lying wasted in the ground beyond the targets.

'The goblins made short work of the elves and their numbers were decimated. Key prisoners were captured and it didn't take Droch long to extract the secrets of Llyn Caigeann.'

'So that was the end of the elfish kingdom,' interrupted Henry, whose voice couldn't hide his feelings of gloom.

'Yes, it was… well, there was another twist,' continued Mrs Wergs. 'The elfish king at the time was called Artan. His wife had just given birth to a son and Droch was anxious to find not just his parents but the child as well. He wanted to stamp out the elfish royal line forever. He tracked down Artan and his queen, but the child was never found. Some say he perished without the protection of parents. But there were rumours that the child's bodyguard showed himself to a human travelling on the road and the child was taken to the other world.'

Henry sat in silence whilst Mrs Wergs brooded over her story.

'I must go, my train is in fifteen minutes,' said Henry, getting up and making for the door. 'It is quite a story, but it's just a… story… a legend. How can I use it in my research? I cannot really put forward a fairy tale!' thinking he was playing his trump card.

'No, there is no proof, there is nothing to prove the story, well...' Mrs Wergs hesitated. 'Well... there is no harm in telling you, it won't come to anything. It was reputed that many, many years ago there was an ancient book written by the elves that chronicled the events I've just told you. But it has never been seen or heard of since.'

'What was the book called?' asked Henry, his hand on the door, impatient to leave.

Mrs Wergs stared straight through Henry as if she had forgotten he existed. Slowly she said, '*The Tree Elves of Ludlow*.'

Chapter 6

Henry got to the station just in time to see his train pull out.

The timetable posted by the station entrance showed that he would have to wait an hour for the next train. *That's a real nuisance*, he thought, and wandered down the platform to an empty bench.

There were only a few other people waiting: a young mother with her baby in a pushchair and a man in a suit walking up and down, talking on his mobile. *I wonder what they would think of the story I've just heard*, thought Henry. *Mad, probably.*

He parked himself on the bench and considered the bizarre woman and her extraordinary story. Her face, when it changed, that was weird or was it his imagination? It had to be; things like that don't happen. The story was intriguing. The cruel outcome of the wedding. That was so terrible it almost had to be true. Funny, though, there was something else that was odd about the whole thing.

Henry's thoughts moved on when he noticed a discarded paper on the bench next to him. *Why do people leave their litter lying around? Why don't they put their rubbish in the bin?*

Then it hit him. There was nothing left lying around Mrs Wergs' house. No bits and pieces, no old newspapers, no junk that piles up. OK, the house was well furnished, his mind now rushing, but it was all so… false!

Instinctively Henry knew he had to go back to number 37 to check that it wasn't all in his imagination. He looked at his watch. If he ran there and back it would take ten minutes. What would he say to Mrs Wergs if she saw him? He would… Henry hesitated, he would ask her… what happened to that special gold mine called Lly… what's-its-name. Had it ever been found?

His mind made up, he ran out of the station, out to the main road and then back into Whitemeadow Crescent.

He cut straight across the village green to save time. As he got closer he was surprised to see an estate agents' 'for sale' board outside number 37. He was almost certain that it had not been there before. He gingerly walked up the short drive, expecting to see the front door open and Mrs Wergs appearing to ask him why he was back. Halfway to the front door he stopped and in disbelief looked either side of him at the long grass that had not been mown for several weeks.

When he had arrived at six o'clock, he was positive that the lawns were neatly cut.

Now standing at the front door he leant over to his left, straining his neck to look into the sitting room. He thought how embarrassed he would be if Mrs Wergs was sitting in her chair and saw him.

'Late to be house hunting,' said a man's voice right behind him. Henry nearly jumped out of his skin.

'You look a bit young as well to be buying a house.' The tone was friendly, and after Henry had gathered his composure, he stood back to see who had given him a fright.

'Sorry,' said the man, laughing, 'I live next door and look after a key for the estate agent. Just keeping an eye on the place, if you know what I mean. Are you interested? Your parents sent you round?'

'No… no,' said Henry, now in a total muddle. 'Oh… actually, yes, they did.' His brain was in shock: he had, less than an hour ago, been sitting in this house with a very strange person, whose face he had seen change and then he had heard an outlandish story about Flora's earrings. And now it looked as if the whole thing had not happened!

'Don't worry,' said the neighbour, 'it's been on the market for some time. Your parents can knock on my door any time and have the key.'

Henry had more than enough time to get back to the station. He walked round by the road, not bothering to cut across the grass. Back on the platform, he made for the same bench. But sitting there were a couple of girls with rucksacks studying a map. He walked past them, deciding he might be asked a tedious question. Standing away from the bench with his hands in his pockets, Henry watched the swallows and house martins cavorting in the fading summer light.

He felt on the one hand that he could now drop the whole silly thing and get on with enjoying the summer and planning his Australian trip. But on the other hand he felt let down. It wasn't that he had been made to look stupid; luckily nobody else would find out about Whitemeadow Crescent. If he had to admit to himself that he was disappointed it was because for one fraction of a second he did believe in Mrs Wergs' story.

The train pulled in to the station. The girls with the rucksacks were dithering by the train door and looking at Henry. 'Excuse me,' the taller of the two said with a heavy Dutch accent, 'is going to Ludlow?'

'Yes, I hope so,' said Henry. 'I don't want any more surprises today.'

*

For the next four weeks Henry was determined to enjoy the summer and made sure he had a full diary. During the day he was either up at the stables with Tom or working at Bensons.

Mr Benson obviously enjoyed Henry's help in the

shop and relied on him as if he had been working for him for some time. As Mr Benson had mentioned when Henry started, he began to teach him about clock mechanisms, the names of the different springs and cogs and how to do simple repairs. Henry was a quick learner and it wasn't long before he was working under supervision on clocks coming in to be mended.

To start with Henry had tried to put the events surrounding Flora's earrings behind him. As far as he was concerned Tom's mother had them locked in the safe. Out of sight was out of mind. But it was easier said than done because he couldn't stop thinking about the book, *The Tree Elves of Ludlow*.

He kept telling himself he was being ridiculous; Mrs Wergs didn't exist. But finding the book became an obsession. The fascination started when he was buying a card in the Castle Bookshop on the Market Square. As he was paying, he made himself ask if they had the book or could they order it for him. The response was a polite shake of the head. On a trip to Shrewsbury with Tom, he made excuses to visit several bookshops. Not long after, he was asked to a party near Hay-on-Wye. Knowing that the town was full of bookshops, he managed to organise his time so that he could make a flying visit around a handful of shops. But all to no avail.

Bookshops weren't the only place he searched. He spent time in Ludlow library and then contacted the British Library, as he remembered his grandfather once saying they registered every book ever published. The answer was always the same: 'Sorry, sir, nothing under that name.' And he spent hours scouring the internet but that drew another frustrating blank.

Despite his perseverance, his investigations revealed nothing. This preoccupation was getting to him and he realised he had to call it a day. The book didn't exist and he had to come to terms with that.

Chapter 7

Henry's visit to Craven Arms was now eight weeks ago and the memories of the events of that day were starting to fade.

It was a nasty, wet Monday morning and Henry had to scurry up Broad Street to avoid the rain. Last week he had agreed with Mr Benson to do a full day at the shop as they were getting behind with repairs. Marjorie was away on holiday for a week and Mr Benson couldn't afford to let his customers down. His reputation would be on the line.

As Henry stepped into the shop, Mr Benson's head appeared from his workshop. 'Morning, Henry, all change, I'm afraid. Mrs Crimps at Castle Lodge has called this morning.' Henry could see by the way that Mr Benson was all puffed up that Mrs Crimps must be important. 'I've been looking after Mrs Crimps and her clocks for years, quite a collection, you'll be impressed,' continued Mr Benson as he filed some receipts. 'Anyway, one of her favourites has stopped chiming and we'll have to go and fetch it. You will see why I need you when we get there.' Mr Benson chuckled and finished off his mug of coffee.

They locked up the shop and hung a sign in the window of the door that said, 'Back in thirty minutes.'

'No coat, Henry?' asked Mr Benson, struggling with his coat as they set off at a brisk pace towards the Market Square.

Castle Lodge stands on the corner of the Market Square and Mill Street. The original house dates back to the early 1570s and its past occupants included important town burgesses who had helped shape Ludlow into a prosperous medieval town. Henry had always thought that Castle Lodge looked an evil place. There was something about the way its roof squatted over its stone and half-timbered walls. The leaded windows were shuttered and lifeless. He had never been inside, but he was sure that it would be dark, cold and its rooms full of secrets.

Mr Benson had no such fears. He knocked on the front door with a customary flourish of his hand. It seemed ages before they heard footsteps. *The hall has a flagstone floor*, thought Henry, as someone approaching to open the door made a crisp, echoey noise with their shoes. Several bolts were drawn back and the heavy door was pulled inwards.

Henry was right. As the door opened, he caught the smell of damp that belongs to a house starved of light and air.

Mrs Crimps stood on the threshold. She was a thin, scraggy woman with lank, cropped hair. Her features were not bird-like in the same way as Mrs Wergs', but they had a hardness that didn't appeal to Henry.

'Morning, Mrs Crimps,' said Mr Benson.

'Don't just stand there getting wet,' barked Mrs Crimps in response, and ushered them inside. Before closing the door she looked up and down the street as if she suspected somebody was watching the house.

They walked down the dimly lit hall, across the flagstone floor to the staircase. Henry was intrigued to see inside the house, although the poor light made it difficult to distinguish any details. The walls were covered in dark and ornate wallpaper, and there were few pictures to look at. They passed a magnificent grandfather clock. On a table next to the clock was a grotesque arrangement of dried flowers.

They climbed the stairs in silence. Henry ran his hand up the highly polished handrail that guided the balustrade in a sweeping curve to the first floor. At the far end of the landing was a large glass case on legs that contained an astonishing collection of stuffed birds. There were all sorts of different species, many that Henry couldn't name. They had been expertly arranged on a branch protruding from a rock face. Every bird was black. *How morbid*, mused Henry.

'Don't touch,' was all Mrs Crimps commented.

Across the landing she unlocked and opened a door, then stood to one side to let them in. The room was a sort of study, well furnished with rugs, comfortable-looking leather armchairs and a sofa that was covered in a dust sheet. At one end was a large fireplace with a stone mantel and the walls were lined with bookshelves. The room had a musty smell and there was a hint of cigars.

Mrs Crimps crossed the room and unhooked a large iron bar that locked the wooden window shutters. She opened the shutters but only wide enough to let in a small shaft of light.

'There she is,' piped up Mr Benson enthusiastically. Henry followed Mr Benson's gaze to a handsome bracket clock sitting on a small shelf high up among the bookshelves.

'I'll leave you to it.' Mrs Crimps disappeared without showing any interest in helping them.

Mr Benson took Henry by the arm. 'Right, time to make yourself useful. See that ladder, bring it round here, could you?'

A library ladder was attached to a rail that ran round the bookshelves, as the books on the top shelves were out of reach even for someone standing on tiptoe. Henry pulled the ladder round and positioned it under the clock. He climbed easily to the top and leant his weight against the top rungs. He stretched with both hands to pick up the clock. But despite his efforts, the clock wouldn't move. Feeling with his fingers, he found that the back feet of the clock were secured by brackets screwed into the shelf on which the clock was sitting.

'Mr Benson, I need a screwdriver, the clock is attached to the shelf.'

'Blast it, I put those brackets there. Why didn't I remember? I will have to go and ask Mrs Crimps if we can borrow one, what a nuisance.' Mr Benson was making for the door, leaving Henry on the ladder. 'What type of screwdriver?' he asked, as he was about to disappear.

Henry strained his neck and used his fingers again to check. 'A normal one, the flat-headed type.'

'I'll be right back. Stay there,' shouted Mr Benson, already halfway across the landing.

Henry relaxed his position on the ladder. He studied the clock more closely and was impressed by its fine face and the pretty walnut case. On either side of the clock were bookshelves holding row upon row of leather-bound books. It was quite a collection and he wondered what the books could be about.

He gazed at the largest book just to the right of him and was at once transfixed. Slowly, he put up his right hand and with his index finger gently traced the faded letters on the spine of the book.

With his finger still on the book he whispered, '*The Tree Elves of Ludlow*.'

All kinds of thoughts flashed through his mind. The story about the earrings, Caled, gold mines, the tragic wedding and why had Mrs Wergs disappeared? Now he had found the book, did that prove they had all existed and Mrs Wergs wasn't a figment of his imagination?

Henry listened for Mr Benson, but there was no sound of his return. Carefully he pulled the book from its shelf and, with it under his arm, stepped down the ladder.

Laying the book on a table behind the sofa and with his ear cocked for Mr Benson's footsteps, Henry opened the book. Knowing there was little time, he turned the ancient pages quickly but carefully. The writing was impossible to read, total gobbledygook. On several pages he recognised an inscription similar to the writing on the sphere of the earrings. At first there was page after page of the indecipherable text and he began to think that the book wasn't going to be of any help to him. He gasped as he turned the next page. The picture was a full-page drawing of Caled's wedding showing the bridal procession pushing its way through the crowd of excited elves. In the distance was the high platform on which could be seen a group of three men. *They must be the King, Caled and Grian*, thought Henry ruefully.

Still alert for Mr Benson's footsteps coming up the stairs, Henry, with more urgency, kept turning the pages. After several more, he came to a picture he hadn't dared hoped to see. Hardly able to control his excitement, he looked down at a drawing of a collection of jewellery. *Probably*, he thought, *the elfish crown jewels*. In the bottom right-hand corner was a detailed sketch of Flora's earrings.

Worried that Mr Benson might be heard on the stairs at any moment, Henry closed the book and made towards the ladder. *Pity there isn't a map*, he said to himself. A map! The word ricocheted around his head. There had to be a map. Risking everything, he returned to the table with the book. There was no map on the inside cover, and as best he could, he flicked through the old pages. Nothing.

Then he heard voices and two sets of feet coming up the stairs.

Quickly he turned to the inside back cover. Again there was nothing. As he closed the book his thumb felt a ridge on the inside. He flipped the back cover open again and ran his finger over the ridge. As he looked more closely, he could see that the ridge went all the way round the back page.

There was something hidden in there. A piece of paper, a picture, a map…?

In the excitement Henry had momentarily forgotten about the voices coming up the stairs. Mr Benson and Mrs Crimps were now crossing the landing and would be in the room within seconds. Hurriedly, Henry closed the book and ran to the ladder, climbing the rungs two at a time. He was sliding the book back into its shelf when the door opened.

'What do you think you are doing?' snapped Mrs Crimps.

Henry pushed the book home and turned round. 'I am sorry,' he replied very calmly, 'I thought if I moved the book it might be easier to get to the back of the clock.'

'You are never to move any of my books,' Mrs Crimps retorted with such venom that it caught Henry by surprise.

'I'm sure he meant no harm,' said Mr Benson, coming to Henry's defence. 'Here's the screwdriver.'

Henry made quick work of freeing the clock and carefully passed it down to Mr Benson.

It had stopped raining when they left the house. They both hurried back to the shop, each with their own thoughts. Mr Benson was keen to get back because they had been longer that thirty minutes, while Henry was trying to collect his wits over the discovery of *The Tree Elves of Ludlow*. It was not just the unearthing of the book. It was getting back to whatever was hidden in the back page. It was obvious that in due course the clock would be mended and then returned to Castle Lodge. If Mr Benson was with him, which was likely, how was he going to have another look without being discovered?

*

The following Friday Mrs Crimps' bracket clock had been mended and was ready to be returned to Castle Lodge.

Henry was working in the shop that afternoon. He heard Mr Benson telephone Mrs Crimps to say that the clock would be back with her by about three o'clock.

'Henry, would you take the clock back to Castle Lodge?' Mr Benson spoke almost apologetically. 'I've spoken to Mrs Crimps and she is expecting you. I'm sure you can manage. It is just that we are up to our eyes here—'

'Yes, yes,' said Henry, interrupting Mr Benson in a rush, 'of course, I'll manage on my own.' He could hardly believe his ears. This was an unexpected solution to the problem!

The clock was carefully placed into a cardboard box with newspaper packed down the sides to keep it upright. Henry set off with the clock under his arm and Mr Benson made sure that he took a flat-headed screwdriver. But once in the Market Square he cut across to Woolworths rather than heading straight to Castle Lodge. He had left a couple of minutes early to ensure he had time to find and make his purchase in Woolies. He asked a shop assistant to help him, but in no time he was out of the shop, his acquisition safely in his pocket, with the screwdriver.

It was precisely three o'clock when Henry arrived at the front door of Castle Lodge. He knocked hard on the door and was surprised when it opened slightly. He pushed it further open, calling, 'Hello... hello, anybody there?' His voice sounded flat in the dark and damp air of the hall.

Hearing no response, he walked in and closed the door behind him. As he got to the bottom of the stairs and was wondering what to do, a side door creaked open, making him jump. Mrs Crimps' silhouette emerged from the shadows.

‘Ah, you must be Henry,’ she said in a disarmingly friendly voice. ‘Mr Benson told me to expect you.’

Henry felt a shiver run through the hairs on the back on his neck. Why was she being nice? Did she suspect him?

‘Help yourself, you know where the clock lives.’ She turned and, still with a pleasant tone, murmured, ‘Let yourself out.’ And like a ghost, she was gone.

She knows something, thought Henry, but Mrs Crimps’ odd charm made him even more determined. Climbing the stairs two at a time, he reached the landing and made for the door to the study. Over his right shoulder he glanced at the strange showcase of black birds.

The study was exactly as before, with the ladder in the same place under the clock’s empty shelf. Without delay, he pulled the clock from its box and stepped up the ladder. The brackets were already loose and Henry slipped the clock easily into place and secured it with the screwdriver. Mr Benson had protected the pendulum with two small polystyrene blocks, which he carefully removed. Remembering his instructions from Mr Benson, he wound the clock, set the correct time and gently pushed the pendulum to set the clock going. The room was filled with the reassuring sound of a perfectly balanced clock.

Henry didn’t even look round as he pulled *The Tree Elves of Ludlow* from its place on the bookshelf. Down from the ladder, he placed the book on the same table and turned to the back cover. From his pocket he tugged out the Woolies bag. Inside was a scalpel with a retractable blade, the sort he had used for model making. Bracing himself, he carefully drew the blade down the long side of the back cover, making sure it was a straight and clean cut.

There was no hesitation or doubt in his actions. His fingers lightly teased out a neatly folded parchment. It was fragile and thin to the point of transparency. Worried by its condition, Henry thought for a second and then pulled out the Woolies bag again from his pocket. Smoothing the bag out, he put the parchment inside and then slipped the bag into the waistband of his trousers, hiding it with his shirt.

Henry was just returning the book to its place on the bookshelf when he thought he heard a noise from the direction of the landing. It had sounded like a bird flapping, trapped against a window. Opening the door onto the landing, he paused, listening for the sound again. Save for the ticking of clocks the house was quiet. Treading lightly, he crossed to the top of the stairs.

Halfway to the stairs, there was a different noise. A sharp, tapping sound from the glass showcase. Stopping, he turned and walked back over to the birds. The bird in the centre of display was a magnificent raven, its head cleverly tilted to one side, as a bird will do when watching something of interest.

Henry stared at the bird and then, to his disbelief, it blinked. Not waiting to see any more, he turned to the stairs. But the moment his back was turned there was a volley of loud taps from the showcase and, as Henry looked round, the glass shattered. The birds, with shrill screams and their wings beating wildly, lifted from their rocky perches and flew straight at Henry.

He was almost at the top of the stairs when the force of the birds hit him. He fell hard against the balustrade but managed to cover his face with his hands. The birds' attack was vicious and their beaks were drawing blood. Several birds were hanging on his chest, stabbing at his shirt. *They want the parchment from the book!* he gasped. Now almost overwhelmed and bleeding badly from various places, he staggered to his feet. Keeping his head down but with a determined effort, he flailed his arms, scattering birds in all directions. Taking his chance, he made the top of the staircase and, sitting quickly on the polished handrail (a trick learnt at school), slid to the bottom of the stairs before the birds could regroup.

Safely at the bottom, he rushed to the front door. Realising the birds were not following him, he stopped to glance over his shoulder. His assailants were perched in a line on the balustrade, their squawks full of anger.

Henry stepped out of the front door into bright sunshine. The relief of getting out of Castle Lodge was so much that he burst out laughing as he crossed over to the Market Square.

Chapter 8

Henry decided that he had better go home first. There was blood on his shirt and his left ear was still bleeding. If he went straight back to the shop his appearance might attract some awkward questions. Besides, he needed to put the parchment somewhere safe.

Arriving home, having ignored some funny looks, he went straight upstairs to his room. Closing the door, he pulled the Woolies bag from the top of his trousers. More than anything else he wanted to have a closer look at the parchment. The suspense was killing him. But if he did… the worry was he wouldn't be able to put it down. He would have to wait. With real willpower, he slipped the bag into his sports holdall that was full of dirty kit. *Nobody will go near that!* he thought.

After a quick shower and a clean shirt, he was off again.

The shop was frantic. It was one of those afternoons when everybody under the sun wanted the services of

Bensons. But it was a blessing in disguise. There were no questions about his visit. Obviously, it was just assumed that the Castle Lodge job had gone without a hitch.

The stream of customers didn't let up until gone five thirty. At last Mr Benson turned the 'closed' sign on the door to face the street.

'You look all in, Henry, you'd better get off… and have a good weekend,' said Mr Benson, waving his arm as a signal that Henry could go. 'Oh, and thanks for taking the clock back to Castle Lodge, very helpful of you.'

Henry didn't wait for any small talk that might prompt a question about his escapades earlier that afternoon. He gave a cheerful 'bye' as he left and within minutes he was back home, opening the front door.

'What are you doing in my room, Flora?' yelled Henry as he got to the top of the stairs, aghast to see his bedroom door open and Flora sitting on his bed.

'I'm just looking through your old CDs as somebody has been borrowing mine without asking,' replied Flora, scowling at Henry.

'Well, it's not me, so can you leave… I've got to change,' Henry added as a further incentive for Flora to get out of his room.

'By the way, Mum washed your very smelly sports kit that you left in that bag,' Flora retorted without making any effort to get off his bed.

Henry tried not to show any sense of panic as he grabbed the bag. It was empty.

‘Flora, I left a shopping bag, a Woolies bag in here,’ said Henry with a slight quiver in his voice, at the same time holding the bag open so that Flora could see inside.

Flora said nothing. With an infuriating smugness, she lay back on the bed, thumping the pillow with her head.

Henry, trying hard to control his temper, walked out of his room but, once out of sight from Flora, went down the stairs two steps at a time. He could hear the washing machine as he raced across the hall and down towards the scullery, which doubled as a utility room. Peering at the glass porthole in the washing machine, he could see his sports clothes whirling round.

Milly can’t have put the bag in there as well, could she? thought Henry in a fit of desperation. He tried stopping the machine, but he didn’t know which button to push or pull, so he gave up and went back upstairs.

‘Is this the bag?’ chirped Flora as a desolate Henry walked back into his room.

Henry lunged at Flora, who neatly rolled off the bed. ‘Must be important.’ She squeaked with pleasure at the effect she was having on him.

‘OK, OK,’ pleaded Henry. ‘Yes, it is important. Can I have it… please… right, what do you want?’

‘You are up to something, Henry,’ said Flora with an edge to her voice that instantly changed the mood in the room. ‘I want to know what is going on. Ever since I bought those earrings, you have been acting strangely, don't pretend you haven't.'

Henry flopped onto his bed, thinking, *How could Flora have picked up on this?* He thought he had been so careful.

'You are right, yes, there is something... odd going on,' he said, 'but you wouldn't believe it if I told you and... if I did tell you, it might put you in some danger.' Henry paused, looking up at Flora, who was watching him expectantly. 'I am not sure, but I think they are stolen and I am just trying to prove my theory.'

As Flora was digesting Henry's response to her accusations, he bounced quickly off the bed, and before she could swing the bag away, he snatched it cleanly from her hands.

'I don't believe a word of that. I don't know why, but I don't,' snapped Flora. 'I've looked in your silly bag and in it was an old map. You're lying, it's nothing to do with my earrings being stolen.' She stormed out the room, slamming the door behind her.

Now at last he had a chance to open the bag and have a proper look at what Flora had said was a map.

Taking his time, he gently eased the map from the bag. He knelt down by his bed, as it was the largest flat area in the room, and opened it out. Although thin, the parchment was in excellent condition. And because it hadn't been exposed to light for hundreds of years, the writing was as sharp as the day it was written.

The parchment was divided into four equal panels, made by the way it had been folded. Three of the panels were covered in close, neat handwriting in a language that Henry only recognised from *The Tree Elves of Ludlow*. The fourth quarter had a carefully drawn map of a piece of countryside completed in the same precise handwriting. Fortunately the map was drawn using symbols, with only a few written explanations. Henry loved maps; they were a bit of a passion in his family. He pored over every detail, trying to understand what it all meant. It was easy to follow a river that meandered across the bottom of the drawing and in two places cliffs were shown running along its banks. The rest of the map was shown covered in a dense forest. Valleys were drawn in to show that the terrain was hilly or even mountainous. There were a number of tracks or paths criss-crossing through the trees. Leading from a point on the river, which Henry thought had to be a ford, was a track along which were notes and directional arrows guiding a traveller deep into the forest. The instructions, which he assumed they were, ended abruptly in a dead end at the top or bottom of a valley. Next to where the track disappeared there was just one word.

One of his knees began to ache. He pulled himself up and stretched whilst still looking down at the map. For a moment he sat down again on his bed, lost in his own thoughts, wondering how he was going to solve the riddle that the map represented.

Suddenly, through his open window he heard Flora outside the house with her friend Tara. It reminded him that he had to find a better place to hide the ancient document, somewhere that Flora wouldn't discover. He listened nervously as they came into the house and up the stairs, and fortunately they disappeared into Flora's bedroom. Not sure what sort of hiding place he was trying to find, he grabbed the parchment and slipped down the stairs. Through the open door of the study he saw the computer, prompting him with an idea. Switching the computer on, he put the document in the scanner and then scanned in each of the four panels. Once they were saved, he protected each file with a different password. Just as he finished, his mobile rang. Tom wanted to meet him for a drink and suggested the Church Inn behind the Butter Cross.

Henry flew up to his bedroom to get his wallet. Still holding the parchment, he looked round his room for another hiding place. It was only a short-term solution; he would choose somewhere safer when he got back. He opened the bottom drawer of his chest of drawers and slid the folded manuscript inside a fleece.

It turned into an impromptu party at the pub, the sort that is a memorable evening without any planning. Tom and Henry got back at midnight, and Henry, without giving the parchment a second thought, fell into bed and was asleep in seconds.

*

Henry woke with a start. It was about one o'clock in the morning. There was a window banging in the wind. Then silence. He started to drift back to sleep, then sat up with a jolt. His window was open and he could tell there wasn't a breath of wind. Struggling out of bed, he reached the window and peered out, at the same time listening for anything unusual. He thought he could detect an odd smell, but after a few minutes, his tiredness drugged his senses. He fell back into bed and was soon asleep.

As Henry slept, he knew nothing of the long bony fingers that walked over him like spiders, expertly tying him up. The small figures that had stolen into his room worked quickly and noiselessly to immobilise him.

Once Henry was bound and trussed, they turned their attentions to searching the room. It wasn't long before they found what they were looking for. Then, as silently as before, they started to lift the still-sleeping figure from its bed.

At that moment Henry woke. He would have screamed, as in an instant he knew he was paralysed. But the scream never came. The nearest figure to him anticipated Henry's reaction and filled his mouth with a gag brought along for the very purpose. The first sensation of paralysis gave way to terror as he took in the small figures moving him, and the powerful stench that he had smelt earlier in the night. The realisation came that there was nothing he could do to defend himself.

Effortlessly, Henry was moved down the stairs and swiftly out of the house. Nothing in the house stirred. Nobody came to Henry's rescue.

The figures paused as a well-rehearsed team before venturing onto the street. Once the signal for the all-clear was given, they slipped into the shadows thrown by the neighbouring houses. Henry had tried to protest several times by writhing and twisting as they carried him. But the vice-like grip of the fingers that dug into his flesh soon made him realise that he was wasting his time.

Now he watched in renewed horror as two of his kidnappers detached themselves and, bending down, pulled up the cover of a large drain and pushed it to one side.

Within a matter of moments, Henry and the goblins had left the face of the earth.

*

It was fortunate for Henry that he wasn't aware that his nightmare was only just starting. The goblins handled him with care, but they were also moving fast, as if they had a deadline to meet. The route began easily enough. The tunnels in Ludlow's old drainage system were high enough for the goblins to stand upright and they could manoeuvre Henry without regularly bumping him. As they progressed, they left behind the brick-lined walls and the tunnel became narrower and the walls rougher. By now the leader of the goblins had removed the gag. Once he was free of the obstruction, Henry vented his anger on his abductors, but his stream of accusations fell on deaf ears. After a bit he appreciated he was better off saving his energy.

Henry quickly lost all sense of time. Earlier, there had been some light filtering down from the outside world, but now it was pitch black. Their path was getting steeper and the walls dripped with water. The air was stifling, making the smell of the goblins even more repugnant. At times the goblins had to get on their hands and knees to push and pull him through tighter spaces. More frequently he cried in pain as they scraped an elbow or shin. But the pace was relentless, the goblins never paused to catch their breath, nor was there any conversation between them. It was as if they knew the route they were taking instinctively.

As time went by, Henry felt that the bindings round his right arm were getting slightly looser. Without attracting any attention, he flexed his muscles so that his bindings started to slip. Now feeling for the first time more positive, he had to wait for the right moment.

Henry felt that they were now deep underground, certainly further than he had ever thought about. Even if he managed to escape, how would he ever find his way out? Would he ever see the light of day again?

At that moment, when his morale was rock bottom, he heard the faint sound of water. As they got closer, the noise of the water increased and Henry realised they were coming to an underground river.

For the first time there was some discussion between the goblins, of which Henry had no understanding. Then two goblins were sent on ahead whilst the rest of the party waited. It wasn't long before they returned and the group moved off again towards the river.

The now-rushing noise of the water told Henry that the river was fast flowing with rough water making regular splashes as it swirled against the rocky sides. The goblins set him down as they stood close to the river organising something that he couldn't see or understand. For a moment he was left alone. Taking his chance, he slipped his right arm out of the bands that tied him. With one hand free, he quickly loosened the other arm so that it too was able to move. Before he had time to undo any more, the goblins picked him up. It then dawned on Henry what was about to happen. They were going to take a boat.

It was more canoe than boat. The shape was long and narrow with only enough room to sit in tandem. The goblins found it awkward getting Henry from the bank into the canoe; he realised they all seemed fearful of falling in and maybe could not swim. As they were shifting him into place, he judged his moment carefully. Slipping both arms back out from the ties, he hit out with all the strength he could muster. His first swing made good contact, catching a goblin fair and square on the nose. There was a cry of pain as the goblin lost balance and toppled into the water. In the ensuing chaos, Henry removed some more of the bindings wrapped round his legs and then, sensing that another goblin was close by, he let fly another strong punch. This time his attack was not so successful. He struck a glancing blow, but the momentum of his swing toppled him forward into the arms of his intended victim. Henry fought to regain the upper hand and was winning the battle for supremacy, when they both fell headlong into the icy, rushing river. Immediately the goblin gave up the struggle, overcome by the terror of water, as Henry had suspected. The goblin's plaintive cries were soon lost in the black swirling waters.

At that point Henry's luck also ran out.

As he and the goblin were sent sprawling into the river, part of Henry's bonds became entwined in the canoe. The goblin leader was quick to take advantage of the situation when he realised that Henry was fighting to free himself. Rallying the other goblins, they dragged Henry back to the canoe, reeling him in like a fish. Unable to free his feet, Henry had to accept that it was becoming a one-sided battle and he was outnumbered.

Exhausted and freezing cold, Henry was hauled by the goblins into the canoe, and whilst several sat on him, the others, directed by the leader, bound him up again. With the ties now cutting into him hard, he was thrown onto the floor of the canoe to lie in the dirty cold water swilling about in the bottom.

Henry couldn't remember the remainder of the journey. The fast-moving river carried the party along for what seemed like an eternity. He was bounced and battered by the rough water until he was sure his bones would shatter.

Then, without warning, the canoe entered a calmer stretch of water and within a few minutes the craft nudged against the riverbank. As the goblins scrambled ashore, from the bottom of the canoe Henry could hear other voices, suggesting there was a reception party waiting for them.

Soon bony hands wrenched him out and he was dumped in a helpless heap on dry land. Lying face down, his vision was restricted, but he was aware of an orange hue to his surroundings. Painfully turning his head towards the growing throng, he could make out a sea of burning torches. The voices he had heard on their arrival turned into a murmur, that gathered in volume as the crowd behind the torches pressed closer to stare at the human creature trussed on the floor.

As he lay there contemplating the end of his world, the leader of his goblin captors loomed over him. The crowd, that was still growing, fell silent as the big goblin pulled a knife from his clothing. Henry caught the flash of metal in the flickering light and, in one last vain attempt to strike his assailant, lashed out with his tied legs. The goblin easily sidestepped the fettered kick and Henry saw the knife glint again before blackness engulfed him.

Chapter 9

Henry felt himself being picked up, shaken by the scruff of his neck and then being made to stand on his own two feet. His mind was still swimming, but he realised that his ties had been cut.

Standing next to him was the goblin leader, still holding the knife that he had used to cut him free. The goblin wasn't leaving Henry's side, meaning that he now had a personal minder. Looking past his new bodyguard, Henry was taken aback to see such a moving mass bulldozing their way towards him. The goblin mob was pulsating with excitement and the noise they made had grown. Many were carrying burning torches, which they waved menacingly in his direction.

Glancing round, he saw that he was standing in a large cavern. The roof was vaulted with an assortment of stalactites that created a cathedral-like air over the seething goblins below. The cavern was bordered to one side by the river, its black, silky waters coated in tiger-stripe patterns made by the shadows of the torches. On the other side, the depth of the cave wasn't possible to gauge, but it seemed to extend indefinitely into the shadows. By a large and distinctive boulder, he noticed that there was an area the crowd seemed to keep free. As he watched, he realised that they were expecting something to appear from that direction.

For the first time since his abduction, Henry was able to study his minder standing a few feet from him. To him, goblins were creatures in children's stories read at bedtime. Never once did he think that they really existed or he would meet a goblin in the flesh.

Compared to a human he was about half the size and his body was all out of proportion. His head was too big for his body. Hairy arms and hands hung as if disjointed from the body. And the feet were misshapen stumps. Henry almost smiled; the goblin was just like a clown. But it was the face that took away any humour. Set off by a dark and oily complexion, the goblin's heavy jowls, hooded eyes and spiky nose were hideous. That wasn't all. The goblin smell, that Henry had first become aware of from his bedroom window, was overwhelming. It was a sickly, rotten stench. Henry felt sick being so close to him.

Henry's study of his captor was brought to an abrupt end when the goblin crowd swung round, turning their attention away from him. There was a rumble of unrest as they faced the area by the boulder that had been kept free. From the shadows emerged an entourage of goblins carrying with them a sense of power. In the centre of the party walked three figures who were taller than the others. As they came closer, Henry could see that these figures were garbed in monk-like habits with hoods drawn up to hide their faces. The other goblins in front and behind wore polished metal breastplates and carried spears. The group stopped short of Henry and from somewhere a bench was produced for the three hooded members of the party.

For a moment Henry was more bemused than frightened by the proceedings. But then he noticed that round the waist of each hooded creature was a thick twisted cord. And at the ends of the two cords was a pair of small silver skulls. As he watched, the skulls started to speak to each other, although nothing he could understand. But they were talking.

Now he started to feel really worried for his safety.

As the hooded figures seated themselves, silence settled across the cavern. Even the skulls were quiet. The central figure of the three cleared its throat and then, to Henry's surprise, started, in a low voice, to talk in English. The voice was only just audible and Henry had to strain forward to understand what was being said to him.

'You are brought before our High Council to answer how you came to be in the possession of this document?' A murmur ran round the crowd as the figure reached inside the left sleeve of its robe. To Henry's astonishment, which quickly turned to dismay, the council leader held the map that he had discovered in *The Tree Elves of Ludlow.*

'I've never seen it before,' Henry said with conviction. Why should he be subservient to these monsters that had dragged him down here against his will?

'Liar,' hissed his inquisitor, leaping up.

The goblins closest to Henry pushed forward aggressively, imitating the hissing sound made by their leader. The rest of the goblin horde jabbed the air with their burning torches and also joined in the hissing, which reverberated across the whole cavern.

The council leader lifted up his arm as a signal and immediately there was silence.

'Nobody lies to the High Council,' said the figure, now hunched back in its chair. 'I shall ask you only once more… where did you find the map?'

'What right have you to bring me here?' shouted Henry. 'I know nothing about the map.'

The mob sensed that Henry was not going to submit and he would fall foul of the council leader's anger. There was little control left in the crowd, but the figure put its hand up once more. The noise level simmered before dying down. The goblins eagerly awaited sentence to be passed on the prisoner.

All three council members stood up. 'You are being very stupid,' mocked the leader, taking a step closer and pointing a finger directly at Henry. 'I need to know,' it said with chilling determination. 'You will be brought to me again tomorrow.' The silver skulls, in support of their owner, started to gnash their teeth as if applauding the performance.

Henry looked defiantly at the hooded face. The leader lifted its head and Henry looked straight into the hood. All he could see was a pair of yellow eyes.

*

The goblins with spears and Henry's minder marshalled him towards the boulder, shielding him from the baying horde that wanted his blood. As they rounded the rock, Henry saw a wide tunnel lit with torches placed in wall brackets every twenty feet or so. As they left the noise behind them, Henry felt the tunnel slope steadily downwards. It wasn't long before they came to a fork in the tunnel and the party paused. There was a brief discussion between the council members, and Henry's guards, after which the guards bowed and the three figures left in a swirl of robes, taking the tunnel to the right. As they disappeared, Henry could hear the skulls chattering away excitedly to each other.

The left tunnel was not so well lit. The guards took several torches off the wall to take with them and then prodded Henry to start walking again. This tunnel was much narrower and there were puddles of rank water under their feet. The route twisted and turned, and several times they went down roughly hewn steps. At the bottom of one such flight of steps, the tunnel came to an end. In front of them was a stout wooden door with heavy metal hinges and a massive lock that gave Henry an understandable sense of foreboding. After several failed attempts to find the right key, the lock was opened and the door pushed inwards.

One of the goblins placed a torch in a bracket outside the door and Henry was shoved through the doorway into a cell. A small bag was thrown after him and then the door slammed to. The clunk of the well-oiled lock was the last sound he heard.

The flames from the torch outside the door spread a tiny amount of light under the doorsill. Henry managed to find the bag and opened it. Inside were a small loaf of bread and a stone flask containing water. He hadn't thought about food since his ordeal had started, but now he was ravenous and quickly finished his meagre meal.

There was little to explore in the cell. The floor and walls were hewn from rock, and apart from the door, there was nothing else to it. The position he found himself started to sink in. He had no way of contacting the outside world. Even if he could call for help, would anybody believe his story? Anyone in their right mind would see it as a joke or a prank and put the phone down on him.

Why had he kept the whole saga to himself? He should have taken Tom into his confidence and then at least they would have supported each other in a situation like this. And Flora knew that something was up. What had been the point of keeping her out of the picture? Henry shook his head at his foolishness.

As his mind wandered over the recent events, he remembered the council leader confronting him with the map. How lucky it was that he had scanned in the document. Thinking about the map, why was it so important to the goblins? Surely the feud between goblins and elves was buried hundreds of years ago? Or was it? For a time Henry was lost in his thoughts, forgetting about his own sorry predicament.

Getting a comfortable position to sleep was impossible. But exhaustion took over and somehow he fell asleep. He was restless as his mind tussled with his abduction. He dreamt he was playing hide and seek with goblins in a forest. His hiding place was impossible to find, but the goblins were getting closer and closer. On the verge of being caught, he leapt from his hiding place only to find that the goblins had vanished amongst the trees. Instead, hanging from every branch, like Christmas decorations, were small silver skulls, laughing at him.

Henry woke abruptly, and despite the damp atmosphere of his cell, he felt hot and clammy. Forest… forest, he repeated the word several times. He felt that something in the dream was trying to reach him. His mind kept coming back to the same thing. The map from the book had to hold the answer.

He was annoyed now that he hadn't studied the map more carefully.

Then in the still small hours, as he lay awake, the answers started to seep into his mind. Like most solutions it was obvious. The forest in the map could be what is now called Mortimer Forest. That meant the meandering river was the Teme. The cliffs along the banks were opposite the castle, which couldn't have been built when the map was drawn. The key question was the path leading from the river. The elfish author of the map wanted the reader to follow the track that led to… what? Henry got up and stretched his stiff legs. He was covered in aches. He had to find that path. But first he had to get out of this hell.

Now he had something to aim for, Henry started to think about his escape. Going over the possibilities, a plan began to emerge.

The torch outside the door had long since burnt out and Henry's watch had been pulled off in the struggle when he tried to escape from the canoe. He hadn't an inkling what time of day it was, let alone the hour. He was hungry again and the cold was getting to him. Then when he was least expecting anything, he heard the slap of goblin feet on the steps leading to the cell.

The cell door was unlocked and two unfamiliar goblins, each carrying a torch, motioned to Henry that he was to follow them. The senior goblin went in front of him and with the other goblin behind him, they set off back up the passage.

Henry's mind was racing, trying to sort out his plan, when he stumbled and went sprawling. He landed with a sickening crash and straight away felt blood oozing down his left knee. As he lay there, his right hand closed round a rock that was small enough to fit perfectly into his hand. His plan changed immediately.

Taking his time despite the impatience of his guards, he slowly pulled himself up, winding up his strength. The goblin in front of him had lowered his torch to look at the wound on Henry's knee. At the moment they both were straightening up, Henry hit him under the chin with all the power he could muster. There was a grunt and the goblin collapsed to the floor.

It took a few seconds for the other goblin to realise what had happened to his fellow guard. Using this to his advantage, Henry quickly picked up the torch lying by the fallen goblin and, with a terrifying battle cry, charged. Not wanting to become Henry's next victim, the second goblin turned and fled back down the way they had just come. Before giving chase, Henry bent down and smartly removed the keys from the belt of the figure lying still at his feet.

It didn't take long before there was a glow from the goblin's torch at the end of the tunnel, next to his cell. Henry stopped, and with the help of his torch he found another loose stone on the floor. With the stone weighing nicely in his hand, he made his way cautiously towards the flickering light. Getting closer, he could hear and see the goblin hopping about and jabbering in terror. Taking advantage of the goblin's distress, he hurled the stone at the cowering figure. It whistled past the goblin's head, missing it by inches, but it was enough to convince the guard that he would be safer in the cell. In a few bounds, Henry was at the door and triumphantly slammed it shut. He put all his weight against the door, found the right key and locked the door.

Henry wanted to slump to the floor and catch his breath. He felt physically and emotionally drained. On the other hand, it wouldn't take long before they were missed. In truth, he would be mad to sit down even for a second. Gathering up his torch, he willed his aching limbs into action.

Further up the passage, Henry stepped over the prone figure of the goblin. He was groaning and holding his head. But he wouldn't be going anywhere for some time. Henry hurried on and in time came to the junction of tunnels where they had parted company from the High Council. The tunnel running to his left was still lit, although every other torch had been removed, meaning there might be some cover of darkness if he took that route. The tunnel to the right led back to the cavern and Henry had no idea if there was another exit that way.

Time wasn't on his side so, with a shrug of the shoulders, he put out his torch in a puddle and turned left. He took his time, peering carefully round every bend. After a bit he gained more confidence and began to quicken his pace. The tunnel floor was well worn and dry, and he was thinking that he would be long gone before they discovered his absence. Just then, he heard voices ahead of him.

Looking round, he saw there was nowhere to hide. He had first hoped that the shadows between the torches could hide him, but now he had second thoughts. The only option was to retreat and take his chance in the cavern.

The cut on his knee was sore, but he managed to break into a painful jog. The voices were still in earshot when he passed the junction and continued on towards the cavern.

The cavern was eerily quiet compared to the last time he was there. He paused by the large boulder, checking for any new dangers. Crossing the open area by the river, where he was paraded in front of the council, carried the greatest risk of being caught. There was no cover to hide behind. Suddenly, the goblin voices behind him sounded much closer, but before he could move, a different party of goblins materialised on the other side of the cavern. Henry wriggled into a crevice behind the boulder, crouching down out of sight. He smiled to himself, despite the added threat; at least he now knew there was another route out on the other side.

The two goblin parties met in the middle of the cavern. There was a heated exchange between them and Henry could only guess that his disappearance was the subject of debate. During the animated discussion, another goblin appeared. Looking out of breath and anxious to speak to the group, the new arrival spluttered out his message. The others listened in silence. As the messenger finished, there was an outcry and an angry stamping of feet. *They're not happy about my attack on their comrades*, thought Henry grimly.

One of the group gave a string of instructions, and to Henry's relief they headed off in the direction that Henry had come from.

Henry eased himself out from his hiding place and with a quick glance round he bent double and ran across the cavern. He had fixed the spot in his mind where the goblins had emerged from the other side and it didn't take long to find where they had come from. Stepping into the new tunnel, he felt his way forward in pitch blackness, hand over hand along the passage wall. The path was sloping down and bending to the left when, with a surge of relief, Henry saw a pinprick of light ahead. With something to focus on, he was able to speed up his progress.

As it turned out the light came from another, smaller cave. Henry kept well into the shadows, every now and again peering out to check for signs of danger. Half a dozen candle-lit lanterns were placed around the cave either on flat stones or hanging from nails. Immediately opposite him was another short tunnel that appeared to lead straight into a second candle-lit cave. All was quiet; nothing stirred. He crossed the first cave and was soon looking carefully into the next one. It too had randomly placed lanterns, but there was no sign of life.

Henry came to several more caves before he found one that was different. Here there were picks and shovels left lying on the ground. In a corner was what looked like an enormous coffee grinder. For a moment his curiosity got the better of him and he stole over to have a better look. In the hopper at the top of the contraption was a pile of broken rocks, and it was obvious that the double-handed wheel to the side was used to grind the rocks to a powder. Underneath was a large sieve and next to it a pile of rough sacks. He was rubbing some of the powder between his fingers that had dropped on the frame of the sieve, when he became aware of the sound of a commotion coming from behind.

Henry didn't wait to find out more. Adrenaline had soothed his stiff limbs and now he tingled with a mixture of apprehension and excitement.

The chain of caves continued, and as Henry moved rapidly through them, there were more signs of activity. But nothing could have prepared him for the sight that greeted him when he rounded a corner.

In front of him was a domed pit at least twice the size of the cavern by the river. The undulating floor was pockmarked with hundreds of small earthworks, each lit by its own flickering candle. Covering the same ground was a seething mass of workers, picking and digging at their holes in the ground with a constant rhythm. Here and there were the same 'coffee grinders' Henry had examined earlier. They were in constant use as they were fed at the top with rocks and the powder was carried away from the bottom.

The racket was horrendous. The screech of shattering rocks, the whirring of the hand-driven wheel and the bone-jarring sound of hand tools crashing against the rocks, combined to make a deafening cocktail of noise.

Henry had no choice. To go back, he would be quickly outnumbered by well-armed goblins. Going forward he might escape in the obvious confusion that his arrival would cause. He took his chance and scrambled down the path leading towards the crowded pit. Almost immediately the workers closest to him looked up and with alarm pointed and shouted in his direction. Henry had not noticed the goblins who were lurking in the shadows. They were guards, watching over the workforce who Henry now quickly understood were prisoners.

For a moment, Henry, the workers and the guards all stood still, looking at one another, uncertain of the next move. The spell was broken by the appearance of the armed goblins who had been following in his wake. At once all the players knew their part. Both the goblin guards and the armed goblins made a beeline for Henry. The workers now understood that Henry was one of them and needed their help. Henry too sensed that the workers had woken up to his predicament and they would come to his help.

Without hesitation, Henry ran into the middle of the dome and the workers closed round him, shielding him from the goblins. The goblins reacted predictably and attacked the workforce, kicking and punching their way through the milling crowd of workers, trying to reach Henry. The whole area was soon filled with thick, choking dust. As candles were knocked over and extinguished, it became harder to see friend and foe alike.

At the height of the melee, Henry felt rough hands pull him to the ground and he was pushed into one of the holes that had been worked on that day. It was a tight squeeze but deep enough for him to sit down in. Then alarmingly earth was shovelled on top of him. To his relief his head was just left uncovered, but a couple of sacks were thrown over him to complete his hiding place.

He lay there without moving a muscle for what seemed like hours. Around him he could hear the goblins restoring order with a ruthless assault on the workers. There were violent scuffles right by his head, but in time they died down and an uneasy silence returned.

Henry counted slowly to a thousand. There was still no sound of goblins so he lifted his head very slowly above the level of his hole. The dome was deserted.

He counted to a thousand again to check that he wasn't going to be ambushed once he re-emerged. But there wasn't a sign of a living creature anywhere to be seen.

Henry heaved himself out of his earthy hiding place. Taking stock of his surroundings, he was on the opposite side of the dome from where he first came in. Hanging around would be a bad idea. If the workers had been taken off somewhere, Henry was sure that the goblins would return to make a more thorough search of the whole area. He decided to work his way anti-clockwise around the perimeter to see if there was another way out.

Sure enough, it didn't take long for him to find a reasonable-looking tunnel with a good path that for once lead uphill. He squatted down by the entrance listening and watching once more to make sure that he wouldn't be followed. As he listened, he heard a faint whimper from an area to his right strewn with smooth, man-sized boulders. He waited and then heard the painful cry again. With the debt he owed to the workers uppermost in his mind, he sprinted the short distance to the boulder field. His search didn't take long. Lying on a bed of sacks was a young girl clothed in dirty rags. She was holding herself and rocking gently from side to side in agony.

When she first became aware of Henry, she tried to sit up as if to escape, but the effort was too much. He stroked her head and the terror in her eyes faded a little. Somehow Henry knew she was dying. He gently clasped her hand to reassure her that he was a friend and with the other brushed the hair from her face. Her composure returned with Henry's soothing touch and a little colour came back to her cheeks. She was fumbling in her clothes and then held out her clenched fist for Henry. Whatever was in her hand, he was meant to take. Opening her hand carefully, Henry found a tiny musical instrument. It was a miniature flute made of ivory and on it was carved a picture that he couldn't make out in the poor light. At one end of the flute was a silver mouthpiece and attached by a ring was a delicate silver chain. At the insistence of the girl, Henry put the flute round his neck. As the flute was slipped over his head, the girl smiled at Henry and whispered, '*Cum ann coem*' (take me home). Her eyes closed and her breathing faded.

Henry let out a deep sigh. The girl had lost her life and it made his problems insignificant. Had he caused her death? If he had approached his escape in a different way, would she still be alive? Henry was sinking under the weight of remorse when the dome was filled by noises he was only too familiar with. But this time the volume was much greater, which could only mean that the number of armed goblins was significantly more than before.

Tucking the little flute inside his shirt, he darted back to the tunnel entrance he had found just before hearing the girl's first plaintive cries. Opposite, he could detect an orange glow coming from the mouth of the tunnel that had brought him to the dome. Then as he watched, armed goblins burst forth, spilling down onto the floor of the dome. They quickly fanned out, ensuring that all the ground was covered. Then a second wave appeared behind as reinforcements.

Henry turned to leave. But one of the lead goblin scouts with sharp eyes had spotted him. There were howls of excitement as the whole goblin company turned and gave chase.

Without much thought to his safety, Henry ran into the tunnel entrance, head bent down and all his senses on alert. For a short time the tunnel ran uphill as he had noticed earlier. Then it levelled out and he could quicken his pace.

The sound of his pursuers was terrifyingly close. Henry started to half run to keep ahead, his entire mind concentrating on the route in front of him.

Then suddenly he was falling through thin air, spinning over and over. The sound of his screams floated into oblivion.

Chapter 10

The shock of hitting the water was one thing, but it was the water's freezing temperature that brought Henry to his senses. As the swirl of bubbles cleared, he instinctively kicked out, climbing up through the bright clear water, using all the power in his arms and legs to break to the surface. Emerging at last from the depths, Henry gulped down lungfuls of sweet air, unable to believe that he was still in one piece.

Treading water, he looked about to get his bearings. He had landed in a lake, which was about the size of two football pitches. A gentle current had eased him off to one side and he was swimming in the flotsam of twigs and larger pieces of wood including a waterlogged branch.

Cliffs circled the lake like a stadium, rising straight from the water's edge and then appearing to arch over. Here and there, growing out from crevasses on the rock face, were small trees, ferns and, in places, curtains of moss hung down dripping with water. The significance of the green vegetation dawned on him immediately. Not only was it light enough for him to see beyond his hands, there, several hundred feet over his head, was a glimpse of daylight. His first sight of the outside world for what seemed a very long time.

Holding on to the floating branch, Henry turned round in the water, trying to decide which direction to take, when a figure appeared on a small shingle beach that at first he hadn't noticed. The figure waved its arms and whistled at Henry as if he were a dog retrieving a stick from the water. Then two other figures emerged and joined in the waving and catcalling.

By now Henry was blue with cold. There was really no choice but to strike out in the direction of the figures. They didn't look like goblins, as the little amount of clothing they had on showed off their pale skin.

As Henry swam closer, he could see that the three figures were all men. As one, they waded out to reach Henry, extending skinny arms to pull him out of the water and onto dry land.

It was hard to tell their age as their bodies were skeletal. Their heads were covered in a thin mat of scrawny hair and their eyes had retreated deep into their sockets. All the while, there was a constant chattering between them that sounded good-humoured and friendly. But to his disappointment Henry couldn't understand a word they were saying.

Standing in his dripping clothes, he grabbed each man's hand in turn, shaking it hard to show his gratitude. The effect on his new friends was more excited chatter, backslapping and beaming faces all round. Henry felt ecstatic. These men were sure to know the way out and before long he would feel the sun on his back and his nightmare would be behind him.

At the back of the beach, Henry could see the mouth of a cave and close to the entrance was a smouldering fire. The three men disappeared, returning with armfuls of dry sticks, and soon the fire was crackling with a good flame.

In front of Henry, the skeletal trio acted out a charade that he quickly understood was their way of telling him to get out of his wet clothes. As he stripped off to his shorts, the three pounced together on the wet pile of clothes. After a playful tug-of-war, Henry's garments were hung on sticks over the fire to dry.

Henry had forgotten about the little flute that was hanging round his neck. As soon as the men noticed the instrument, they inquisitively drew nearer to him for a closer look. Henry already had an emotional attachment to the flute and held up his hand to put off any ideas of examining his gift from the dying girl.

Out of his dripping clothes, Henry at last stopped shivering and his skin started to regain its normal colour. His next dilemma was how to ask for some food to eat; he felt ravenously hungry. Tapping on the shoulder of the nearest man, Henry pointed at his mouth and rubbed his tummy. Henry's acting produced gales of childish laughter, but to his relief all three nodded in understanding and disappeared again into the cave. On their return they carried between them several fresh fish, which they threaded onto more sticks and placed over the fire to cook.

As the fish cooked and Henry warmed himself by the fire, he had a chance to study more closely the three men squatting in front of him. They certainly weren't goblins but didn't look like humans either. Whilst they were painfully thin, Henry could see that their features were delicate and they carried themselves with a gracefulness that he had not seen before. What really set them apart were their eyes, which were almond-shaped, and their colour was a penetrating pale blue.

The man in the middle looked to be the strongest of the three and probably the leader. Henry nicknamed him 'Jim'. The one on Jim's left was the thinnest, so he was christened 'Slim'. The last man, Henry nicknamed 'Dim', for no particular reason other than that it rhymed with the names of the other two.

Jim was checking the fish and decided that the smallest one was cooked. He handed it to Henry on a flat stone. On another similar stone, Slim piled some vegetables that looked like green shoots. Henry didn't waste a moment. He started to pull off pieces of fish, wolfing it down with mouthfuls of the green shoots. They tasted out of this world, better than any gourmet dish he could remember. It wasn't long before he was picking over the bones left dangling on the stick. Feeling ready for the next fish, Henry threw the fish bones onto the fire and was turning over the stick in his hand, when he noticed that it wasn't a stick at all. It was a long thin meat bone.

Glancing up at Jim, Slim and Dim, Henry saw all three momentarily had a totally different expression on their faces. It reminded Henry of three vultures waiting to feed on a rotting carcass.

Henry held up the bone like a piece of evidence in court. 'What is this?' he said sharply, adding in the same breath. 'Where did this come from?' Henry wasn't really sure what the thinking was behind his questions. But all of a sudden he felt distinctly uneasy.

He got up from his position by the fire and walked over towards the entrance of the cave. Slim, Jim and Dim got to their feet in unison and rushed in front of Henry, trying to block his way. The three of them were laughing and talking nervously as if to make light of the situation. Henry brushed them aside and stepped into the mouth of the cave.

Once his eyes had become more accustomed to the dark, he could see the cave was a reasonable size with dry walls and an earthen floor. In one corner was a pile of driftwood that had been collected from the lake and dried for the fire. In the furthermost corner was another pile that on first inspection looked like another assortment of dry sticks and logs from the lake. Jim, Slim and Dim were now silent, standing in the cave entrance, wringing their hands and muttering to each other. In the poor light, Henry used his right foot to explore the pile. Then, with a sickening feeling in the pit of his stomach, he bent down to scrutinise the centre of the heap more carefully. Unmistakably, it was a pile of bones, and staring back at him were four human skulls.

*

Henry whipped round to confront Jim, Slim and Dim, but they had vanished. Running out of the cave, he could see no sign of them at first. Then, hearing voices above his head, Henry looked up to see the three men following a path that clung to the cliff face as it wound its way above the lake. The path was no more than a thin ledge, hardly discernible against the rock wall and patchy vegetation. Henry started looking for the path to give chase but somehow the way had been cleverly hidden and he soon gave up. All he could do was watch as the men disappeared round a buttress of rock.

Henry sat down again by the fire and stared into the glowing embers. He felt exhausted. All he wanted was to get out of this never-ending nightmare.

He knew he had to think about the pile of gruesome bones. What did they mean? Originally had there been a larger group of people and the three men were now the only ones that had survived? Yes. And those who had died… had they died of starvation because there was no apparent way out? *Poor devils*, thought Henry, and even though his outlook was bleak, he felt happier with his explanation.

There was no sight or sound of anyone on the cliff path. While he had the place to himself, Henry took the chance to have a better look inside the cave. Returning to the stack of bones, he searched about for anything else unusual. Feeling with his hands and fingers as his eyes got accustomed to the light, he explored the nooks and crannies along the cave wall. The area to the left of the bones drew a blank. He switched to the other side and almost straight away his hand closed on a small bundle wrapped in a piece of hessian.

To see what he had found, Henry walked out of the cave and started to unravel the bundle. Kneeling down, he spread the contents on the ground by the fire. There were three small knives that looked home-made with rough wooden handles. Henry rubbed his thumb across the one he had picked up. Its blade had only just been sharpened and would cut through anything like butter. The other item in the bundle was a hand axe. It too had a wooden handle fashioned out of a good piece of wood. The metal head fitted onto the wooden shaft and was bound tightly into place with twine. It was razor sharp too and as a weapon it would be lethal.

Henry rolled up the bundle and returned it to the place where he had found it. For a moment he stood again over the bones. Slowly he reached down and pulled out one of the skulls from the bottom of the pile. He held the skull in the palm of his hand, then turned it over. The area that had been the back of the head was missing. Henry rang his finger alone the jagged edges of the gaping hole. There was no question that a heavy blow to the head had killed the unfortunate owner of the skull. No doubt the owners of the other skulls had suffered a similar fate.

Henry threw the skull back onto the pile. Walking out of the cave, he took several deep breaths to calm his nerves. Why would Jim, Slim and Dim want to kill the others in their group? Or were the victims people like him they had first rescued and then killed? It didn't make sense. Henry walked to one end of the little beach and climbed onto a rock that protruded out over the water. If there wasn't enough food to go round and they couldn't find a way out… then getting rid of a few weaker members would be a horrible option but nevertheless a possibility. *But… but*, contemplated Henry, *why keep the bones?* Surely they would get rid of all the evidence of the bodies, not keep the remains lying around. Then it dawned on Henry.

He jumped down from his position on the rock and ran back into the cave. He gathered up an armful of bones and returned to the beach. In a frenzy he examined the bones one by one, then flung each bone far out into the lake. All the bones had the same telltale cuts and scrape marks.

Henry sank to the ground, putting his head into hands. He had escaped from the clutches of the goblins only to be rescued by three cannibals.

*

Henry didn't brood long over his predicament. He started walking up and down the beach turning over his options, if there were any. To control his frustration he picked up a stick from a pile by the fire and flung it as far as he could into the middle of the lake. He watched it circle lazily in the eddies then it pirouetted smartly and disappeared. Strange. Henry threw another stick to exactly the same place. The stick completed its dance routine and again disappeared. Now intrigued, Henry climbed back on top of the rock that protruded out over the lake. Choosing a larger, heavier stick, he lobbed a well-aimed throw and the stick landed perfectly on target. From his slightly higher position he could clearly see the stick revolving and then, like the others, vanish.

Henry laughed. The current in the middle of the lake had to come from and go somewhere. There wasn't any evidence of a surface channel for the water, meaning the water flowed underground, perhaps to another cavern? He did have an option now! It might be very risky, but was it a way out? With a grin, he knew there was only one way to find out.

Henry waded out from the same point that he had been pulled from the water. He let out a whistle, having forgotten how cold the water was. He was just about up to his waist when he heard a shout from the cliff path. Looking over his shoulder, he saw Jim, Slim and Dim returning, carrying bundles of the green shoots. There was more shouting from Jim and then Slim detached himself from the group and hurried down ahead of the others.

That confirms it, thought Henry. *They must know that a secret way out from the lake does exist. And Jim has told Slim to stop me from finding it.* Slim was now close to the end of the path as Henry launched himself into the chilly waters. He put his head down and swam to the area that he had hit with his sticks. As he reached the spot, he looked back to watch Slim start to lower a rope ladder. The ladder tumbled over a short cliff and Slim began to descend towards the beach.

So that is how they do it, said Henry to himself, and without further hesitation he ducked down, diving for the bottom of the lake.

As the water was crystal clear, he had no problems getting his bearings. With a thrill he could see the stony bottom of the lake and the water flowing smoothly into a black gaping hole. Now certain of what he had to do, he would surface for a full intake of air then dive back down in a bid for freedom.

But looking up towards the surface, he was alarmed to see Slim's legs treading water above him. Henry kicked hard, propelling himself up through the water as fast as he could, aiming directly at the swimmer. Slim was caught completely by surprise as Henry grabbed both his legs and yanked him underwater. Slim gasped with the shock of being pulled down and swallowed mouthfuls of water. And whilst he was fighting to gain control, Henry pushed him even further underwater until he could put his foot on Slim's head, giving him another shove towards the bottom.

Henry arrived on the surface to catch his breath just as Slim neared the bottom. With a few seconds in hand, Henry steadied himself, breathed in deeply several times and dived again, slipping past Slim, who was disorientated by Henry's attack. Skimming along the bottom, he quickly reached the black hole, which was wide enough for him to swim straight into. It all happened very quickly. For a second he was plunged in darkness. Terror engulfed him. Would he ever come out alive?

As quickly as it had started, his brief panic came to an abrupt end. As he swam through the tunnel Henry could see bright water ahead of him. With a couple more strokes he found himself back on the surface looking at a different lake. Its shape was longer and thinner than the one he had just left. Above, the same cliffs, covered with vegetation, soared over his head, allowing daylight to filter down.

He swam to the edge of the lake and pulled himself out of the water onto a rocky outcrop. Quickly recovering his breath, he realised that the whole escapade had only taken a few seconds. He shook his fist at an imaginary audience, relishing his triumph at getting a step closer to freedom.

Taking stock of his new surroundings, he picked up the noise of fast water at the far end of the lake. As he adjusted to the sound, he realised that there were rapids ahead or, worse still, a waterfall. Henry slid back into the water. Sticking close to the side, he worked his way down to the far end of the lake. As he swam, he became more aware of the current gaining in strength and a rumbling noise ahead. If he wasn't careful, the current was going to pull him from the relative safety of the water's edge.

Henry paused and tried to fight his unease. Casually he glanced behind him. To his disbelief, Slim was swimming straight for him, holding a knife between his teeth.

There was nowhere to hide. Henry pulled himself half out of the water. Coiling his strength and judging his moment, he sprang forward, pushing off from the side to give himself extra power. The heel of Henry's right hand hit Slim in the mouth, half knocking the knife from his teeth. The blade caught the side of Slim's face and blood gushed out over both of them. Henry felt the current drag them downstream and he knew there was little time before they were both swept into the unknown. Slim recovered quickly. Grasping the knife before it was washed away, he lunged at Henry's body. The blow was only at half strength, but it hit Henry in the chest, causing him to double over in the water with pain. Unbeknown to both of them the blade had struck the flute, which had rolled the thrust away, causing only a shallow flesh wound. Henry felt his chest and realised how he had been saved. Then on the spur of the moment he chose to pretend that he was in much more serious trouble. Slim circled, looking for the killer strike, but mistakenly relaxed his guard momentarily. Henry once more gathered every muscle in his body and swung his elbow back, hitting Slim on the side of his head. The hit could not have been more damaging. Slim lost all his senses for a few seconds and the current, now much stronger, pulled him away from Henry. Seeing his advantage, Henry put every last ounce of his dwindling energy into reaching the side of the lake and grabbed a handhold amongst the vegetation to stop himself following Slim.

Slim came round, but the current was now his master. He wasted the last of his strength by thrashing about with his spindly arms. Then he was gone, swallowed up by whatever lay beyond the thunderous noise of water.

This time it took longer for Henry to catch his breath and recover from the ordeal. And he was frozen to the bone. Thinking about it, he knew he had no alternative but to retrace his route through the underwater sump. Then there was the question of dealing with the other two when he got back.

Gradually he pulled himself upstream away from the faster water. The hard work and concentration numbed his sense of cold and pain. Arriving back at the top of the lake, he steadied himself for the return dive and was relieved to find it an easier experience the second time. Henry told himself that once he had emerged back into the first lake, he would have to take his chances as they came.

Breaking surface, Henry couldn't believe his luck when he saw there was no sign of anyone on the beach. So as to avoid attracting attention, he swam slowly to one side of the shore and pulled himself up to lie on the shingle. He lay there for a full five minutes watching and listening as well as enjoying the gradual return of some feeling to his body. Smoke was drifting up from the fire and his clothes were still draped over the sticks to dry. There was an eerie calmness. And still no sign of the other two.

Watching the area in front of him, his mind was jolted by the memory of the rope ladder that was the means of reaching the cliff path. There was no indication of the ladder, but it had to be there, hidden amongst the rocks.

With a renewed purpose, Henry got to his feet and, treading carefully over the shingle, walked towards the fire and the mouth of the cave. As he crept forward, the sound of snoring came from the cave. *Is my luck now really turning?* thought Henry. Standing close by the cave entrance, it was obvious that Jim and Dim were napping. All he had to do was cross in front of the mouth of the cave and find the rope ladder.

Passing the fire, Henry collected his shirt and trousers and tucked them under his arm. Tiptoeing, he crossed in front of the cave. Nobody stirred. Once across and safely out of sight, he allowed himself to relax for a moment, leaning his back against the cliff to steady his nerves. It didn't take him long to find the single rope pushed deep into a crevasse that ran down from the top of the cliff. Once the rope was free, he gently pulled it, anticipating that the ladder would follow on down. The rope snagged after a couple of pulls. Giving it a harder tug, Henry was caught off guard when the ladder came clattering down on top of him. The noise sounded like gunfire. He froze, every sinew in his body alert to danger.

Sure enough the snoring stopped and there were mumbled voices from inside the cave. Henry moved closer to the entrance and flattened himself against the rock. The voices stopped, and Henry could detect that either Jim or Dim was shuffling sleepily towards the front of the cave to find out what all the commotion was about.

It was Dim who appeared. He stretched and yawned as he looked around, half expecting to find Slim returning with his prisoner. He waited a few more seconds, but there was nothing to see. Slim had always got his man before. He would be back in due course. He and Jim might as well continue their sleep before the feast later that night. Turning to go back inside the cave, his eye caught sight of Henry's foot protruding from his hiding place. Thinking that Slim was playing a trick, Dim sidled over and bent down to pinch his toe.

Henry was ready for any eventuality, but he wasn't expecting his toe to be tickled. As Dim appeared in front of Henry, both looked at each other in astonishment. But Henry was the quicker of the two to act. He slammed his hand over Dim's mouth and twisted him to the ground, at the same time putting his knee into the small of Dim's back. He whimpered pathetically but offered no resistance. Henry used his shirt to gag him, binding the sleeves tightly round his head, making it impossible for Dim to make even the slightest sound. Henry then hauled him to his feet. Looking directly at Dim, who was shaking with terror, Henry drew a finger across his own throat to show the consequence of any ideas of escape.

Henry pointed at the rope ladder and signalled to Dim to start climbing. Somehow they both managed to climb up with Henry hard on Dim's heels. There was little to worry about as Dim seemed to be incapacitated by his capture. *Perhaps Dim was the right name for him after all*, thought Henry.

Once they were both on the narrow path, Henry pulled up the rope ladder and put it out of reach. He undid the single rope from the ladder and wound it round his waist for possible use later. Henry put his trousers on and then beckoned to Dim to start moving up the path. But Dim wouldn't move. He had sunk down on the path in a dishevelled heap, immobilised by Henry's threat to cut his throat. Henry pulled him to his feet and shook him hard to get some sense into him. This only made matters worse. Dim recoiled in fear, lost his footing on the path and fell backwards. He toppled over the edge, landing at the base of the cliff with a sickening crunch.

Henry didn't wait to see Dim's fate. The noise would have surely woken Jim. He started up the path at his second attempt of finding his way to freedom.

The path was narrow but proved to be easy going. To begin with it traversed above the lake. As it gained height, the path turned away behind the buttress of rock that Henry had seen the men disappear behind earlier. Winding through a cutting, the sides of the path were overgrown with vivid green ferns and spongy mosses. Henry recognised, mingled in with the lush vegetation, the clumps of the green shoots that he had eaten with his fish. In places, water seeped out of the rock face and collected in small clear pools. Now and again, Henry stopped and cupped his hands to drink and splash his face with the cool water. Coming out of the gully, the path rejoined the side of the cliff. Here the surface of the path became more treacherous. Small, loose stones made the going slippery. Ignoring the risks, Henry hurried on, using his hands to steady himself as he scrambled higher and higher above the lake.

Then, without warning, the path petered out. Henry cursed in frustration. Looking up he calculated he was less than a hundred feet from the top and freedom. His only option, it seemed, would be to climb the last section. He glanced down over his shoulder at the lake shimmering several hundred feet directly below. If he fell it would be a long way down. *It's not worth thinking about*, he thought, and started off.

The first section was a scramble, using both hands to grip rock, branches and vegetation. After a while, he found a safe ledge on which he could rest and look ahead to plan the next part of the route. Straight above him was a pitch of bare rock about twenty or thirty feet high. There was no way round and it would have to be climbed. Once over that, he would have to make a simple traverse over a steep grassy bank. Then he would be on the home straight. A vertical fracture in the rock, perhaps just wide enough to climb up, looked as if it might lead to the top.

Wiping his hands on the back of his trousers, Henry started up the rock wall. Without pausing or looking down, he moved steadily upwards, always keeping three points of contact on the rock. There was no shortage of handholds and he kept up an unruffled rhythm to the top. Elated at keeping his nerve, Henry pinned himself, just below the grassy bank, in a convenient cleft of rock. The grassy bank looked relatively simple, although it was steeper than he had first estimated.

Eager to get on, Henry stepped onto the bank and gingerly started working his way across hand over hand.

Twice he felt himself slip, but he had good handholds and was able to quickly check his position. With a sigh of relief, he reached the bottom of a rock fracture. Without resting, he clambered into the bottom of the crack and prepared himself for the final ascent. As he surveyed the route above, a sound carried up on the air from far below. His body went rigid as he strained to hear the noise again. Was it Jim coming after him? Nervously, he scanned the ground below him. For a while he sat quite still. Nothing disturbed the silence.

Henry had to think about his next move very carefully. He put his back against one wall and, bracing his legs against the opposite wall, he was able to shuffle up the fracture. He dragged his bottom up the rock no more than two feet. Then it was the turn to move his feet up a few paces. And so on it went. To begin with, the width of the fracture was perfect for this method. In a few minutes, Henry was halfway up and for a blissful moment he caught the sun on his face.

What he hadn't seen from the bottom was the funnel bulging in the middle before getting gradually narrower at the top. He was now stretched fully across the width and any more progress using this way of climbing was beyond him. His left leg started to shake with exhaustion and he felt a tinge of panic. He moved down a few feet to get a better purchase against the wall with his feet and backside.

He hadn't forgotten the rope tied round his waist. Fumbling with jittery fingers, he undid the knot and pulled the coils free. Above him but out of reach was a stout-looking shrub growing out of a crevasse. Feeding one end into his belt, he bunched up the rope and threw it over the shrub. It took two more exhausting attempts to get the rope to fly over the shrub and the other end to land back within Henry's grasp. But at last it worked and he pulled the rope down so that it was securely round the shrub's trunk. With the two ends now hanging down, he knotted them together to create a loop that he could stand in. Could the trunk take his weight?

Hanging on to the rope and trusting to his luck, he managed to first get his knee into the loop and then, with a struggle, he stood up with both feet in the stirrup made by the rope. The trunk sagged but held. Henry calculated that he would need to complete three more similar manoeuvres before he could crab up the last bit of the funnel. But above him there wasn't another tree or shrub that might be strong enough for his purposes.

Up to his left was a crack filled with dark earth and small rocks. With one hand he brushed out the dry peaty soil around the biggest stone that had become firmly lodged. Once he had got his fingers right round the back of the rock, Henry undid his trousers and, after a few awkward moments, pulled them off. Next he threaded one trouser leg through the crack, behind the jammed rock and out again. Balancing in his rope sling, he knotted the two trouser legs together to make another loop.

Henry pushed his left hand into the same crack and, twisting it, locked it into place. Then, taking some of his weight on his left arm, he inched himself up with his right hand pulling on the rope. Trembling from the exertion, Henry dragged his left knee into the trouser sling and allowed it to take his weight.

Now the rope was free to be used again. He had to rest for a moment. Sweat was pouring down his face and his hands were slippery from repeatedly wiping the drips from his eyes. Using his sleeve he dried his forehead and wished he could have a drink of water.

Searching for the next and hopefully last secure point, his heart leapt when his fingers closed over a solid handhold. Beyond it was another equally good hold and suddenly Henry had left his trousers and rope behind and was able to straddle the fracture with both legs. His energy returned and with growing excitement he slowly edged his way up using arms and legs to at last reach the top.

Henry's hands and then his arms emerged from the hole, grasping and pulling at great tufts of grass. Pushing the last few feet with his legs, he eased the top half of his body out into warm bright sunshine. Lying there, still only half out of the hole, he drank in all the pleasures of being alive, rubbing his face in the damp green grass and feeling the novelty of a breeze ruffling the back of his head. It was a full five minutes before Henry was ready to pick himself up and think about getting home.

As he finally pulled himself up, a hand seized his ankle and started to pull him back down into the hole. Henry screamed with the shock. Jim! Jim had followed him right the way up to the top. It was Jim he had heard.

Henry jammed his legs hard against the side of the funnel to stop himself sliding any further back. Looking down, he could make out Jim's grim face in the shadows as he worked to dislodge Henry's footholds. Growing over the entrance to the fracture was a clump of hazel. Henry lunged for the nearest branch, which he bent down and snapped off with a ferocious twist. The result was a sharp stick with a splintered end. Henry looked down again into the hole. Jim's head was bent down, so all Henry could see was a matted head of hair. Bracing himself against Jim's continued assault on his footholds, Henry shouted at Jim with a deliberate tone of panic and despair. Thinking he was winning the struggle, Jim looked up. At the same split second, Henry stabbed the hazel twig into Jim's left eye. Immediately, Henry felt Jim's hand fall from his ankle. Then came a piercing cry of pain and terror. Jim's hysterical shouts faded, ending in a faint splash as his body hit the lake far below.

This time Henry scrambled right out of the entrance to the hole. Walking away, he couldn't control a sob that was a mixture of disbelief and relief at surviving. He didn't know which direction he was heading in, but all that mattered was he was going home.

Chapter 11

Henry's journey home was straightforward compared to his ordeal at the hands of the goblins and his escape from the cannibals.

Without his watch, he had no idea about the time of day, but it felt like early evening. Even in the weakening light it didn't take him long to find a forest track, which in turn led to a metalled lane. Coming across the lane lifted his spirits and he made good progress along its way. His luck stayed with him. As the lane crested a hill, he could see the lights of cars cutting across open countryside on a main road.

Standing on the junction of the lane and the main road, Henry tried in vain to flag down a lift. *It's hardly surprising*, he thought to himself. *Who would stop for somebody only in their underwear!* Eventually a car pulled up a little way past Henry. He chased after it, getting to the driver's door as it came to a halt. The driver, an elderly man with his wife sitting beside him, lowered the window and looked in sympathetic horror at Henry.

'Thank you, thank you,' blurted out Henry. 'I can explain, you see, I have been dumped, I don't know where, after a stag night. My trousers, wallet, have all gone. Please can you give me a lift?'

The woman's hard expression immediately softened. 'Oh, how mean of them,' she said. 'Let him in, Donald. Where did you want to go, where's home?'

'I need to get back to Ludlow,' replied Henry with a plea in his voice.

'Oh yes, well, we are heading for Leintwardine. But I am sure we can make a small detour, Donald?' answered the woman. 'Go on, open the door, Donald dear, let the young man in.'

'Thank you so much, thank you,' mumbled Henry as he climbed into the back.

As the car pulled away, the warm interior and the soft seats acted faster than a tranquilliser. He rolled over and was fast asleep before his head hit the back seat.

The next thing Henry felt was a hand shaking him awake. 'We're here, my friend, this is Ludlow,' said Donald kindly.

'Will this be alright?' added his wife, looking over her shoulder at Henry, who was still semi-drugged with sleep. It took him a moment or two longer to grasp where he was, but the familiar shape of the Butter Cross was right outside the car window.

'You have been so kind, thank you for going out of your way,' said Henry in a voice weighted with relief.

'Not at all,' said Donald, who was interrupted by his wife.

'Yes, glad we helped you out,' but with a snort she added, 'No more silly pranks, though!'

Henry watched the car turn and disappear down Broad Street. Following in its wake, he wearily crossed the road and headed too down Broad Street to number 44.

Henry knocked on the door, having lost, amongst everything else, his key.

'Oh, hello, Henry,' welcomed Tom's mother. 'What on earth have you been up to this weekend, or shouldn't I ask?' she said with an understanding giggle.

'No, don't ask,' said Henry with a charming smile that put an end to the matter.

'OK, but Henry, you know I don't normally go into your bedroom, well, I did because one of your friends rang and wanted to leave a message. Your room looked as if it had been ransacked. I've tidied it up but… please, well, you know what I am going to say.'

'I am really sorry,' said Henry, who had quite forgotten what the goblins had done to his bedroom. 'It won't happen again.' And he planted a small kiss on her cheek to make doubly sure he was forgiven.

'Actually, I have got a big favour to ask you,' added Henry as he followed Milly into the kitchen. Opening the fridge, she found a bottle of white wine and poured two glasses, giving one to Henry.

'You look as if you might need this… go on,' she said.

'Would you mind ringing Mr Benson first thing in the morning and say that I will be off sick for at least a couple of days?' Henry's voice trailed off at the end as he saw her expression. As a second thought he continued, 'I cannot tell you why just yet… please.'

'Go to bed,' said Milly, laughing.

*

Henry didn't wake until past eleven o'clock the following morning. He slipped downstairs to make a cup of tea. Filling the kettle, he spotted a scrawled note on the kitchen table to say that Mr Benson was sorry to hear that Henry wasn't well. He hoped he would be better later in the week. At the end of the note was a large exclamation mark.

He took his tea up to bed and went back to sleep.

It was well into the afternoon when he woke again. This time he felt wide awake and refreshed. He lay in bed for a few more minutes, staring out of his window, his mind swimming with his abduction. The goblins were after something that must be important. Would they risk showing themselves to the human world to steal the map unless there was something exceptionally important at stake?

Suddenly, without warning, he felt downhearted. Was it mad to go on with this whole nonsense? Did he really need to put himself in this danger? And in any case, it was all so far-fetched. He sat up, and as he did so he felt the little flute round his neck. Up until now he had not had a proper look at the instrument. Holding it closer to the light of the window, he studied the tiny carved scene for the first time. He touched its soft silver mouthpiece and instinctively he knew he had to go on. If nothing else, he had to fulfil the girl's dying wish to take the flute home.

The plan that had been lurking in the back of his mind suddenly came to life. He jumped to the window. His alarm clock said it was nearly four. Looking out of the window, he saw that it was going to be a lovely warm summer's evening.

There didn't appear to be anybody else in the house as Henry switched on the computer. Within a few minutes he held a printed copy of the map in his hand.

After he had got some clothes on, he wrote on the bottom of the message from Mr Benson that he was going for a bike ride. As a further thought he added he would get fish and chips on his way back for his supper. The tyres on his mountain bike needed a bit more air, and then he was off, first heading down Broad Street, over Ludford Bridge and up the other side towards Mortimer Forest.

It was a long hard pull up the hill, but Henry felt revitalised after his long sleep and with the plan bouncing about in his head. Working hard, he continued the climb, soon passing the Forestry Commission buildings before coasting down the other side towards the picnic area.

In amongst the scattered picnic tables there were still a few ramblers and mountain bikers. They were packing up their equipment and finishing off the remnants of their picnics before turning for home.

Choosing an empty picnic table well away from the others, Henry took a seat to inspect his map. He had been biking several times before in Mortimer Forest and could remember the general layout of the tracks. As he tried to orientate himself with the map, he quickly realised that tracing the original track would be a mammoth task. But undeterred, he decided to follow the forestry roads to the highest point by the Forestry Commission watchtower. From here he would be able to look over the forest to see if he could identify any likely routes that the old track might have taken.

The forestry tracks were wide and easy to follow. Within twenty minutes, Henry was standing by the watchtower, casting his eyes over the blanket of woodland that rolled away on all sides of him. In truth it was impossible to make any sense of where the route up from the river might have come. There were too many possibilities. To start with, should he spend some time in the library studying the ancient maps for clues? Happy with this plan, Henry set off on the return journey.

He had noticed, on his way up, an intriguing track that had been used by mountain bikers. It took a direct route straight downhill to the bottom, cutting across the main track several times. Descending steeply, it weaved its way down through the trees and over some challenging obstacles. He had to give it a go. He freewheeled slowly on the main track until he found the starting point. Pausing, he checked that it was heading in the right direction and then launched off down the first section. It was far harder than it first looked. The track made his bike behave like a bucking bronco. The first time he crossed the main track he needed a minute or two to catch his breath. Setting off once more, the narrow track ran steeply down through more open woodland. His speed picked up and the bike rattled and banged its way over ruts and roots. Henry saw the turn ahead too late. Despite slamming on the brakes, he and his bike somersaulted over a bank of bracken and tumbled down the other side into a shallow ravine.

Henry laughed at the exhilaration of his crash. He brushed off some dirt and was none the worse off except for a few scratches. Fortunately the bike had landed well away from him and looked in one piece. But something was digging into his foot. Sitting down, he removed his shoe and quickly found a thorn that was the culprit. Glancing about him as he pulled his shoe back on, he noticed that he was sitting overlooking a well-worn footpath that ran along the bottom of the ravine. He slithered down the few feet until he was standing on the path. Below him the pathway went round a corner and then seemed to disappear into a thick belt of trees that hung like a curtain across the path. Puzzled, Henry walked towards the belt of trees. Pushing aside the drooping branches, he peered in. The interior was dark, the closely knit trees allowing just a small amount of daylight to filter down. But there was enough to see some way. A short distance ahead was a gap in the trees, where the path emerged on the other side.

It was too hard to resist. He pushed his way through the trees and walked out to the other side.

*

Henry was greeted with a surprise. In front of him was a broad, open valley. On either side tall grasses covered the gently sloping sides. At the top of each side, woodland curled over to meet the meadows. And through the soporific haze of a warm summer's evening, he could see more woods stretching into the far distance.

The grassy slopes were alive with wildflowers: poppies were sprinkled far and wide, buttercups and knapweed daubed yellow and violet patches across the landscape. A dragonfly hurried past and a pair of red admirals sunbathed by the path. Henry felt entranced and, without thinking, he followed the pathway that meandered down the valley through the meadows.

Next to him he heard the burbling of a spring and, following the sound, he found the water filling a shallow stony basin. Kneeling on the grassy bank, Henry washed his hands, which were still covered in mud from his bike crash. Then he drank the cool, crisp water to quench his thirst.

Henry sat back and soaked in the dreamlike scenery. It was strange that he had never seen or heard of this valley before. As he sat and watched, he was sure he heard the faint sound of bells. Standing up to get a better bearing on the sound, Henry saw a large herd of goats drifting across the valley. They were white, the colour of lemon sorbet. In the middle of the herd was a handsome billy goat, showing head and shoulders over his females. And he was clearly bringing his herd towards Henry.

The bells grew steadily louder and it wasn't long before a sea of goats surrounded Henry. The billy goat kept his distance, but the others were friendlier and came to nudge him as if asking to be stroked.

Feeling it was time to go, Henry got up and began to walk back to the path. But the goats circled tightly round him, not letting him reach the path. He wasn't afraid, more curious, when shoulder to shoulder the goats began pushing and guiding him down the valley. It became obvious they were taking him somewhere.

As they all moved down through the valley, the herd fanned out with Henry placed in the middle. The billy goat walked just behind him and he could feel the goat's eyes in his back. Escaping wasn't on Henry's mind. But even if it was, somehow he knew it would be futile. At the bottom of the valley was the vast expanse of woodland that Henry had seen when he had first cast his eye over the land. As the pathway approached the trees it swung left to follow along the edge of the woods. On the bend, the leading goats left the path and headed straight in under the trees. The whole herd trotted on, following in the footsteps of the leaders.

They had walked into a beech wood with an open forest floor. Above them, the sun's rays were still strong enough to cut through gaps in the high canopy. In the contrast between sunlight and shadow, the tall smooth grey trunks of the beeches looked like the columns of an ancient temple. In the stillness, Henry had never seen anything as magical.

Crossing a stream, the trees changed from beech to oaks. But these were no ordinary oaks. Their trunks were as wide and tall as a block of flats and their branches interlocked overhead like a network of aerial roads.

At last they came to a glade and the goats stopped to graze the grass. They ignored Henry, who sat down with his back against an oak. He wondered in the gathering dusk when he was going to get home. Though this time, unlike his other adventures underground with the goblins, he felt unafraid and still more than curious.

*

He must have nodded off for a few minutes. He woke with a jolt at the sound of children playing close by. Not moving so as to avoid frightening anybody, Henry watched as four children tumbled and rolled about between the trees. Suddenly their shouts and giggles stopped and they stood up quickly to brush down the twigs and leaves from their clothes. Henry's eyes searched between the trees to see what had interrupted their play.

Then he saw the figure of a man standing by the children.

The man strode over in Henry's direction and the children followed, the youngest holding the man's hand. The man was bareheaded and wore loose-fitting clothes of green, with gold embroidery around the collar of his shirt. Around his waist was an ornate belt and from it hung a sword.

His eyes were pale blue and his fair hair was shoulder-length. The smile chased away any doubts that he could only be a friend.

'I am so pleased you have come at last, Henry,' said the man, holding out his hand. 'I am Owain, Prince of Gwydden, son of Gruffydd, protector of the elfish kingdom. But,' said the man, 'my family and friends call me Min.'

Chapter 12

Henry's mouth opened and closed. 'How on earth did you know my name?' asked Henry with disbelief.

'We have been expecting you,' said Min as he turned and picked up the child that had been holding his hand. 'Let's get you home, Fingel. Come on, Hebe, Oscar and you, Merlin. Your mother will be worried.' The other three children trotted happily after Min. After deliberating momentarily, Henry followed on too.

'Where am I?' called Henry.

'Come on, surely you have guessed by now,' said Min without looking over his shoulder.

Henry stopped. 'I have no idea. A herd of goats brought me here, which is bizarre, I admit. But I haven't a clue where I am or what is going on.'

Min then stopped too. He walked back to Henry. 'I am sorry. You are in the elfish kingdom of Gwydden. But we don't have much time. I will explain later. Follow me.'

Henry was about to say that he had never heard anything so ridiculous but decided to keep quiet. It was incredible, but the strange man with a sword had a magnetism that Henry found difficult to ignore.

Min and the children disappeared round behind a particularly magnificent oak. When Henry caught them up, they were starting to climb a staircase hewn from the inside wall of the hollow tree. Like the stairs in a castle turret, the spiralling treads were well worn in the middle by the passage of feet. Henry ran his hand along the polished trunk walls, worn by elfish hands that had smoothed the rough wood as they steadied themselves as they climbed higher. At the top, the stairs opened onto a platform between the massive boughs. And from where they stood, Henry could see there were several more staircases that led in different directions. The stairs were more like ladders, which curled and twisted round the girth of branches and disappeared up amongst the leafy tops of the trees. Fascinated, Henry followed Min and the children as they climbed one of the ladders. Those in front scampered up, but for Henry it was a new experience. It was difficult to get a rhythm especially when he dared to look down to see the ground between the branches a long way below. The cheeky faces of the elfish children were peering down at Henry when he arrived at the next platform.

Standing behind them was Min, who gave Henry a hand to pull him up to join them. There was only one way forward from this point, which was over a rope bridge. With an encouraging wave from Min, Henry was made to cross first. Looking straight ahead, he wobbled across with Merlin laughing at his heels.

Looking about him, Henry couldn't hide the smile on his face; scattered across the tops of the oak forest was a village of tree houses. They weren't easy to see. More cottage than house, each blended in amongst the trunks and branches using oak timber with bark left on the outside. Canopies woven from grass shielded doors and windows, and the roofs were all neatly tiled in bark. Some cottages fitted snugly into the fork of the tree whilst others, which looked grander, were built so that branches protruded out of the roof and extra rooms jutted out on balconies. From some of the dwellings a wisp of blue smoke curled skywards, dissipating amongst the greenery above. And in the gathering dusk, lights winked through the leaves as the elves settled down for the evening.

Henry watched rooted to the spot as elves left their firesides, appearing outside their front doors to point and chatter excitedly at the approaching visitor.

Between each house, rope bridges or ladders criss-crossed the treetops to join the village together. Min now took the lead. As they crossed another bridge yet more smiling, waving elves gathered to watch the party go by. Ahead, Henry could make out in the gloaming a house that was bigger than any of the others that he had seen. With two storeys, the structure clung to its tree like a swarm of bees with branches poking out in every direction, its ancient roof sagging so much it seemed it might slide off at any time.

In a moment they reached the strange house and there to greet them was a group of four elf elders. They bowed deeply in front of Min, who patted each one affectionately on the shoulder.

'Henry let me introduce you to my most trusted and loyal aides, Bàn, Srad, Turlach and Cùlag.' Standing behind Henry, Min whispered in his ear, 'They too have been waiting a long time for this day.'

Henry shuffled forward, receiving a bow from each elder, although not as formal as the bows made to Min. Cùlag grasped Henry's hand after his bow, squeezing it hard, happiness and relief showing in his old eyes. Min gently guided Henry to the front door, from which spilled a warm yellow light. Crossing the threshold, they passed through a hall hung with tapestries into a large comfortable circular room. As expected in a house made of wood, beams stretched across the ceiling. Henry noticed that they were carved the length and breadth with details of the elfish way of life: hunting, fishing, as well as archery and elfish games. In a corner, part of a trunk was built into the room, its bark stripped off and the surface decorated with more carvings depicting battle scenes.

In the middle was a log fire, its red embers throwing out some welcome warmth. The sweet-smelling smoke coiled its way lazily into the rafters and out into the approaching night. Around the fire cushions of every shape and size were strewn across the floor to make one continuous couch. The room was lit by candles arranged in ornate lanterns that dangled on long gold chains from the beams. And in the candles' shadows, Henry made out more wall hangings showing deer and wild boar.

It was a welcoming, cosy room made for gatherings, feasts and for talking long into the night. Henry felt drawn into its fabric and at home.

Min unbuckled his sword belt before throwing himself down on a pile of green and crimson cushions with patterns picked out in gold thread. The elders followed suit and sat two either side of Min.

'Now, Henry, let's get you comfortable,' started Min. 'We have got a bit of ground to cover before the night is out, but before we start, are you hungry?' Henry sunk into some deep cushions close to Min, and with the mention of food, he realised he was starving.

Min clapped his hands. From doors hidden from view elves appeared, wearing royal livery. Low-level tables and simple wooden bowls were placed between them. Henry watched as platters piled with cuts of venison, wild boar and smoked eel were brought to them. Each plate was decorated with wildflowers, blueberries and tiny strawberries. Baskets of warm bread appeared and elderflower wine in silver goblets.

Just as Henry thought he couldn't eat another morsel, royal servants appeared again carrying honey

cakes and mead in pretty horn cups. Despite his groans of protest, he was made to tuck in once more.

After the last remnants of food were taken away and the tables removed, Min cleared his throat and a more serious mood settled over the company. 'Henry,' Min started as an expectant silence settled over the room, 'as I said earlier, we have been expecting you. The elfish people have been awaiting your arrival from the human world for years... yes, for hundreds of years, I suppose.'

For a second, Min was distracted by his own thoughts, then continued, 'Ever since the death of King Cleddau and his son Grian at the fateful wedding, the elfish nation has suffered and dwindled at the hands of the goblins. From our defeat at the Festival of Corran and the capture of our last gold mine, Llyn Caigeann, the goblin empire has gone from strength to strength. You see, Henry, over the centuries we have been hounded and beaten to near extinction. But... but we hope you, Henry, are our answer. I, we, the elfish nation need your help.' Min paused and took a sip of his mead as he looked directly at Henry.

'Have... have I been... set up?' asked Henry.

'Yes and no,' responded Min with a grin.

Henry looked over his shoulder, feeling a greater presence in the room. He hadn't heard anybody move behind him. But crammed into every part of the room, he could now see the solemn faces of elves standing alongside each other, hanging on every word spoken.

'But before we go on,' continued Min, 'I want to hear what has happened to you since the earrings were found in Ludlow. It's important to us.' Min turned to the elders, who all nodded in agreement.

'Did you somehow… plant the earrings?' questioned Henry, still feeling that he had been used.

Min nodded. 'Yes, we did. A huge risk, I know. They could have fallen into the wrong hands, but against all the odds, the plan has worked… so far!'

'What do you mean?' exploded Henry. 'I have been kidnapped by goblins and nearly eaten by cannibals. For me, your clever plan has wrecked my summer. And you are still talking about using me. I need an explanation… now!' A murmur rippled round the room as they recognised the anguish in his voice.

'I understand,' said Min gently, 'but whatever you think, you are now part of our struggle against the goblins.' Min pointed straight at Henry. 'You cannot escape from it, this is your destiny… I am sorry. We do need your help. The elfish nation won't survive without it.'

The room stirred as the mood became more serious.

Min went on, 'Please tell me what has been happening to you. I have heard you have been through a lot, but I want to hear it from you… from the beginning.'

Henry sighed. Looking into the embers of the fire, he realised that Min was right. He had to explain what had happened to him. Maybe it would help him avoid falling victim to the goblins again.

'Alright,' said Henry.

He began by telling them about the job with Mr Benson. How Flora had brought the earrings into the shop after buying them from the craft fair. His search to discover more about the earrings and finding Mrs Wergs. Henry repeated everything that Mrs Wergs had told him: the history lesson, the tragic wedding and her belief that the earrings were made by elves. When he mentioned her yellow eyes, Min jumped up, cursing into the air, the words making the audience gasp.

'You know what she was, don't you, Henry?' spat Min. 'A goblin!'

'But she told me about the book *The Tree Elves of Ludlow*,' Henry half whispered.

'I know. She was playing with you. She wanted you to lead her to the book and particularly the map.'

Henry went on to tell them about the discovery of the book and his return to Castle Lodge to find the map.

Min slapped his thigh and laughed when Henry described the birds in the glass display cabinet breaking out and attacking him. 'They really were making it difficult for you! Keep going.' Min chuckled.

When Henry started on his kidnap by the goblins, the elves shifted restlessly and Min with the elders became agitated.

'They understand what I am saying?' asked Henry, nodding in the direction of the circle of faces around the room. Min pointed to a corner of the room where an old elf smoking a long pipe was sitting cross-legged. Beside him two boys were scribbling hard in leather-bound books. 'He knows your language and has been interpreting. The boys are keeping a record. On with your story,' Min said grimly.

Henry carefully retraced each step of his ordeal at the hands of the goblins. At times he felt a chill in the room and his voice echoed as if he was speaking alone. He felt the hairs on his neck tingle as he spoke of the workers in the dome who had hidden him. But the most difficult part to tell them about was about the dying girl. Min was biting his lip when Henry told them of the girl's final request.

There were angry mutterings from the gathered elves as Henry's near disaster at the hands of the cannibals reached their ears. But as the story unfurled, the warmth returned to the room as everyone savoured Henry's escape. By the time he was telling them of his return home and his resolve to keep going in order to fulfil the girl's wishes, Henry was their hero. The euphoria nearly became a riot as elves pushed forward to touch Henry and share in the legend that was unfurling in front of their eyes.

Min stood up, reaching for his sword and belt. Banging the floor with the scabbard, he brought order to the room. Addressing the eager throng, Min's voice

carried with it the excitement of the evening. 'Hold firm, steady your nerves. Tonight, right here in our midst is the young man sent to us as promised by our forebears. Yes, this is the first day of our fight to win back all that we have lost to the goblins. But we have a long struggle ahead; this is only the beginning of the beginning. Go home, spread the word and be ready when called.' Turning to Henry, Min winked and said quietly, 'Follow me.'

*

They left the house, leaving the elves aflame with anticipation, taking a different bridge and several ladders before they descended a spiral staircase inside another oak. As they reached the bottom of the steps an elf in uniform stepped out of the shadows. Henry shouldn't have been surprised, but her long fair hair seemed out of place with a gold breastplate, a sword at her waist and over the shoulder a long bow and quiver. After a brief consultation with Min, she snapped her fingers and three more identical warriors appeared with sturdy-looking ponies, all with bridle and saddle. Thrown over two of the ponies were long thick cloaks, one of which Henry was only too glad to accept.

'Can you ride? Too bad if you cannot,' Min joked.

'Second nature.' Henry laughed as he swung into the saddle on a sturdy little grey. 'Are you taking me back?'

‘No. We haven’t finished yet,’ said Min, now serious. ‘I need to take you to somewhere important. When we get there you will understand. Then you must get home.’ The party set off with two warriors in front and the other two following in the rear. In the middle Henry and Min rode knee to knee, in silence, deep in thought.

The moon was up. The forest, drenched in thick shadows, shielded their passage. They skirted glades where pools of platinum moonlight beckoned the unwary. Henry felt that they were being watched every step of the way by unseen eyes.

The bodyguards and the ponies never faltered in their direction or pace. Henry drew his cloak round him, feeling the night’s chill. They began to climb through pine forests, the floor littered with boulders, some as big as houses. They weaved their way between the rocks and, before reaching the top of their ascent, they left the cover of the trees.

Under the starry sky Henry felt less intimidated. But Min drew close to Henry and under his breath he told him to keep his eyes skinned. ‘Now we are out on the moor we are in much more danger. It is possible that some goblins have infiltrated this part of our land.’

For a while the pace didn’t alter. The party moved swiftly, contouring the rolling heather, keeping in dead ground but always climbing.

Approaching a hidden dip, the front warriors stopped and dismounted. Min too slipped out of his saddle and motioned to Henry to do the same. The two warriors from behind joined them and took their ponies. The other two he posted as sentries, their bows strung and arrows at the ready. With a 'follow-me' nod from Min, they both moved forward out of the protection of the hollow. By Min's example, the pair ran crouching across an open stretch of heather.

Henry nearly lost his footing as the ground suddenly fell away and they tumbled down the short steep slope of a large hollow. It was a perfect circle in shape and in the middle was a hedge of gnarled and twisted mulberry trees, planted too in a circle. Together they reached a wooden gate that swung easily when Min pushed it open. Stepping into the sanctuary, Min bowed his head and, speaking softly, uttered, Henry assumed, an elfish blessing.

Min now took Henry by the arm and led him into the centre of the circle until they were standing on an ancient slab of stone. Min sat down cross-legged and wrapped his cloak tightly round himself. Henry understood he was to do the same. Between them was a word carved into the stone. Below it was another smaller word. Min traced the lettering with his finger and leant forward to be closer to Henry. 'This is the grave of King Cleddau; it is also where his son Grian is buried. I had to bring you here because it is written in our elfish law: where the elfish empire died, so it will be reborn. And that place is here.'

Taking both of Henry's hands, Min continued, 'You remembered King Artan; Mrs Wergs told you about him and his fate at the hands of Droch.' Henry felt the electricity through Min's hands and he couldn't speak. 'Artan and his queen both were killed, but their son survived. We know he reached your world safely. And we know that he prospered, raising a family, and died in his bed.'

Henry felt he knew what was coming next.

Min went on, 'The elfish royal line still exists but in your world. We need it back here to lead us against the goblins.' Min looked hard at Henry. 'The heir to the elfish throne is alive and living in Ludlow.' Min looked up at the clear night sky and back at Henry. 'Please, Henry, the elfish people need you to find him and bring him back home.'

Min let go of Henry's hands and sat back.

After a long silence Henry got to his feet. 'How did I walk into this place? What made me walk into your country?' he asked quietly.

'The girl who gave you the flute, she was my sister. She crossed to the human world to look for our king. But the goblins somehow got to her first. She was imprisoned along with many other elves to mine gold for the goblins, our gold in Llyn Caigeann. The wearer of the flute has the power to move between your world and our world. So, you see, the flute would have given the king safe passage back here.'

'I'm sorry,' said Henry. After a pause he went on, 'There is one other thing, why was I nearly eaten by cannibals who were more elf than goblin?'

Min winced. 'Yes,' he said, 'they must have been elves that had escaped the goblins. I should think they were recaptured and in exchange for their lives they were made to be guardians of that escape route. They caught any elf that managed to get away and to survive… well, you know the rest.'

Henry sat down again in front of Min. 'When I was given the flute by your sister I was afraid that I had been responsible for her death. I told myself I would fulfil her dying wish to take her flute home. And here it is.' Henry lifted the flute from round his neck and placed it in the palm of Min's hand. 'But,' continued Henry, 'I didn't say I would bring your king home. No, I cannot do it. The whole thing is absurd. I want to go to Australia, if you know where that is. Sorry.'

Henry got up and turned to walk back towards the gate. There was no sound of Min following him.

He walked defiantly through the gate and then over the open space they had earlier run across. As he approached the dip in the ground where the ponies were hidden, a noise came from behind that sounded like Min catching him up. Turning to speak to him, it was the smell that warned him and made his blood run cold. Three goblins rose out from the heather, their yellow eyes glowing. As the blades of their swords flashed in the moonlight, he saw they were already dripping blood. Henry stumbled backwards as they swept down on him.

But he neither heard nor saw the arrows before they struck all three goblins between the eyes. Then strong hands picked him up, dragging him into the dip, where the ponies stood waiting motionless.

'Let's get you back before you get us all killed.' Min's voice was harsh. The remaining two warriors bundled Henry into his saddle and with Min in front they took a different way off the moor.

Henry didn't remember very much of the journey back to the valley which he had walked into that same summer's evening. The ponies, under Min's direction, galloped through woodland, over streams and open meadows. Always behind them were the female warriors protecting their backs from further goblin attacks.

At last Min slowed to a trot and Henry recognised the track leading up to the curtain of trees that he first came through. A short distance from the trees they stopped and Henry turned in his saddle to thank the warriors who had saved his life and protected him on the way back.

But there was nobody behind him.

'Where are the…' started Henry. Min said nothing. Then Henry understood. They wouldn't be coming home.

Min jumped from his pony. 'That's your path. Good luck.' Min saluted Henry and turned to mount again.

'Wait,' shouted Henry, 'I will do it, I will find your king and bring him home.'

'Why?' snapped Min.

'Because if they gave their lives for me,' said Henry, pointing back down the track, 'I am ready to give my life to find your king.'

Min stepped closer to Henry and once more took his hands.

'Thank you.' Min's smile changed everything. 'Here, you will need this,' slipping the chain with the flute over Henry's head. 'Get as much help as possible, try your family, any of your friends. But I will also send you someone to help you. Someone special.

'Just one more thing,' added Min, 'be careful who you let play the flute, but that will be explained later.'

'How will I know who it is?' Henry asked, now feeling the weight of his new responsibility.

'You will know, you will know,' said Min, laughing as he turned his pony towards home. 'Now you had better get going.'

Chapter 13

Dawn was breaking as Henry left the belt of trees behind him. Finding his bike was a relief, and after checking it over, he clambered back up onto the track, pulling the bike with him. With more care, he started down the mountain bike trail, zigzagging through the trees until he came to the next forest road. Anxious to get home without any more mishaps, he abandoned the trail for the forest road and headed for the picnic area from where he had started the previous evening.

As he checked his bearings, his eyes caught some movement in the trees above and to the left of him. He freewheeled slowly forward to get a better look. The early morning light was still poor, but he could make out first one then several dogs. To begin with he thought they were dogs. The pack, which grew quickly to thirty-odd, was standing watching him. There was an air of danger about their behaviour and Henry started to pedal faster to pick up speed and get past them. A cold, haunting howl ricocheted through the trees and, as if it was an order, the dogs moved quickly down onto the track. It was then that he realised they weren't dogs at all. It was a pack of wolves.

There was no way round the wolves. There were too many to plough straight through. They would make mincemeat of him in seconds. Henry slowed to a halt about twenty yards in front them. Every wolf was looking directly at him, watching his every move. And as they circled about on the road, the pack was moving slowly closer and closer to him.

This, thought Henry to himself, *is a bit like the goats*. But the wolves were not coming to him to be stroked. Thinking of the goats prompted him to touch the flute hanging round his neck. He had never tried to play a note on the instrument before, but without a thought he put the flute to his lips. Strangely no sound came from the flute. But the effect on the wolves was miraculous. With yowls of pain, they turned and fled into the trees, where they were soon lost to sight.

Henry shook his head in disbelief. Not only was that a narrow escape but also the flute clearly had some other powers.

Henry put his remaining energy into getting back to the picnic area and the road just beyond. Reaching the main road was a relief, and without stopping to rest, he tackled the climb to the top of the hill. After which he could coast all the way home.

He let the bike gather speed after reaching the top, feeling the damp air of the dawn rush over his face. But a sense of foreboding overtook him as his mind ran through the strange events of the night. And the reception by the wolves was a warning. It meant that he was being watched at every move. The goblins had to be behind it. It also supposed that the goblins knew about the elfish king living somewhere in Ludlow. Min was right… he was in the middle of it all and there was no escape.

All was quiet when he stole up the path to number 44. He pushed the bike into the shed and let himself into the house. There was another note on the kitchen table. Mr Benson was expecting him in the shop at one o'clock.

*

The afternoon in the shop was a struggle. Business was quiet and Mr Benson was engrossed in repairing a clock that was on its last legs. It seemed like a lifetime to five thirty.

Between fighting to keep awake and serving the customers, Henry had been going through his mind about who to recruit to help him find the elfin king. The obvious choice was to talk to Tom and Flora. But what would they make of it? He could just imagine the scope for remorseless teasing round the breakfast table for months to come. If he did let them in on the secret, he would need some cast-iron proof. Where would that come from? Then there was the question of the 'helper' that Min had promised. How would he know who it was? Would 'it' have pale blue eyes, fair hair, perhaps carry a bow and a quiver of arrows? More to the point, how long would it be before he showed up?

Mr Benson hardly looked up when Henry said he was off home.

After he got back, Henry was feeling fidgety and needed something to do. Still curious about the old map, he decided to go to the library. It was just beginning to rain as he left the house. It was the first subtle change in the weather. Autumn had crept into the air.

Reaching the library, Henry asked for help at the desk and was quickly pointed in the direction where the maps of the local area could be found. Before long he was poring over all sorts of ancient maps spread out over a wide table in the reading area. He was fully absorbed when he heard a familiar voice behind him.

'Hi, Henry, what are you doing here?' asked Flora, sensing immediately that Henry was up to something again.

'I'm doing some research, that's all,' Henry said in a guarded tone.

Flora slipped into a chair opposite him. With her elbows on the table she put her chin in her hands and looked directly at Henry.

'I know you are up to something, Henry. First it was the earrings and then that map I found in your bag. You got your knickers in a right old twist when I hid it from you. And remember, you tried to put me off by telling me that the earrings had been stolen and you were in some sort of danger. I didn't believe a word of that either.' Flora finished by reaching over the table until her face was just a few inches away from his.

'Go on, I dare you… tell me,' challenged Flora.

Henry felt he was trapped, but then as his mind raced he thought this might not be the way he planned it, but it looked as if she wasn't going to be so easily fobbed off this time.

'Alright,' said Henry. 'I'll tell you. I am only telling you because I need your help. But, and it is a big but, you will have to listen to the whole story without interrupting. And at the end of what I am going to tell you, there is no ducking out. You will be in it up to your neck. This isn't something you can take or leave. Understand?'

Flora nodded. 'I'm all ears.'

To begin with Flora listened attentively. But as the story went on she became more distracted until with a jolt she suddenly said, 'I'm sorry, Henry, I really, really didn't think you were going to tell me a fairy story. I thought this was going to be about someone… well, the earrings had been stolen as you told me. Then after some clever detective work you had worked out who had nicked them… that sort of thing. Not elves and goblins… come on!'

‘It’s the truth, this actually happened to me. I am not making it up,’ retorted Henry crossly.

An elderly man at the other end of the room looked across at them. ‘Couldn’t you two find somewhere else? This is meant to be a quiet area, didn’t you know?’

‘Come on,’ said Flora, ‘let’s go.’

Outside the library, they crossed the supermarket car park and cut through Attorney’s Walk onto Corve Street. Henry was fuming. The gamble of telling her was a disaster; he should have listened to himself. How was he going to stop Flora telling everybody and making him look ludicrous?

‘Flora, how about a cup of coffee? We can nip into the Bull Hotel.’ Henry thought it was worth one more go and a drink might make her more receptive.

Just at that moment Flora’s mobile rang. ‘Hi, Tara, yes, OK…’

Henry waited patiently whilst Flora chatted away to Tara. Then he realised that it was one of those calls that went on and on, probably about nothing. Without saying anything he left Flora to it, disappearing up High Street, back to Broad Street and down to number 44.

*

Several days later Milly said at breakfast that she had a surprise announcement to make. Her business had had a record year and had won two more awards that had really put her on the map. To celebrate she would take them all out to dinner at the best restaurant in Ludlow a week on Friday. Tom gave his mother a hug and Flora gave a whoop and then went upstairs muttering that she would need something new to wear.

'Henry, you will come too, won't you?' asked Milly anxiously.

'I would really like to, thank you, but I was meeting a friend in Shrewsbury after work. You've met Charlie; I'm going to Australia with him. We've got to fill in some forms.'

'Well, that won't take long. You could meet us at the restaurant? The table is booked for eight. Please, I would love you to be there with us.' Milly sounded adamant and Henry had heard that the food was wonderful.

'That's really kind. If I get there at about half past eight, would that be OK?'

'That's fine.' Milly nodded.

Henry was pleased. He felt it would be a good night out.

*

Fourteen guests in all were asked to the party, and everyone in Ludlow seemed to know about it.

For the rest of the week the conversations round the kitchen table centred on the menu and the choice of wine. Everyone had his or her view, but in the end, to avoid a family row, it was agreed to leave it all to the chef, Claude, who, after all, was the expert.

On Friday morning the house was in a state of excitement. Flora had got round her mother and was going to pick up her new dress that afternoon. Sitting down to breakfast, she was in an upbeat mood. As Henry cleared his plate and was about to leave for work, Flora couldn't resist asking him what he was planning to wear for the party.

'I bet you are going to come as a little green el—' Flora smirked.

'Shut up, Flora,' snapped Henry, anticipating her dig at him. He stopped her short with a stare that could have turned her to stone.

'Flora, you are being a pain,' joined in her mother. 'We will see you later, Henry,' she added as he headed for the door.

*

The restaurant was at the bottom of Corve Street. Run by a French chef and his English wife, it had earned itself quite a reputation in just a few years with locals and visitors from all corners of the country. As Henry's train pulled into Ludlow from Shrewsbury he was looking forward to the evening. Several friends had told him that it was some gastronomic experience, but he never thought he would have a chance to try it for himself.

The evening would also take his mind off the elfin king. It was over a week since he had returned from his adventures in the Kingdom of Gwydden and already he was beginning to wonder if he had dreamt the whole thing. Flora's reaction had got to him. Her belittling jibe was painful.

If Flora had reacted with such disdain, how would Tom react if he tried to tell him? But he now had an obligation to Min; it was a commitment, which meant he had to do something.

And so it went round and round in his mind.

Henry pushed open the restaurant door just after eight thirty. Stepping into the reception, all the complicated thoughts that had been dogging him vanished. A lively fire was burning in the grate. By the thick tapestry curtains was a sofa and a couple of deep armchairs arranged by a low table. Across the room was a discreet bar, behind which was a display of old-looking brandies and malt whiskies. The elegance and furnishings of the panelled room gave him a reassuring, welcoming feeling.

Seated on the sofa, a young couple looked up from studying their menus. They both smiled at Henry as he stood for a moment wondering what to do.

Just as he was about to flop into one of the armchairs, the chef's wife appeared at his elbow. 'You must be Henry? Let me take your bag and then you can join the others who are round the corner waiting for you.'

‘OK,’ said Henry, hearing the babble of party talk coming from inside the restaurant.

‘Will you have a drink? …It’s champagne,’ asked the woman, offering him a glass on a silver tray.

‘Mmm, thanks.’ Henry took a sip then a longer drink as he decided it was just what he needed. Following the directions, he ventured further into the restaurant and peered round the corner. Several faces turned and beamed at him as he sought out Milly.

‘Oh, well done, Henry, you made it in good time and you’ve got a drink, good.’ She put a hand on Henry’s shoulder and guided him towards her other guests, introducing him to those he didn’t know.

‘Hi, Henry, good to see you.’ It was Tom who drained his glass and reached for another from a tray sitting on a side table. ‘How did it go with Charlie?’

‘Oh, fine, just glad to get the forms done and in the post. You should come too,’ added Henry, but he knew Tom had other plans.

‘I suppose I could join you later, I have thought about—’ Another guest pulled him away before he could finish.

Henry could hear Flora’s voice, but she was talking to the Unwins, who ran a local publishing business. She was just out of sight behind them and he had to manoeuvre himself to join her.

‘Hello, Henry,’ said the Unwins together.

‘Hi,’ said Henry before turning to Flora, half wondering what her new dress looked like. His smile faltered as he took in what she was wearing.

'Flora, what on earth are you doing wearing those earrings?' Henry's tone was hard, but he kept his voice low so as not to involve the others.

'Why not? They're mine.' Flora shook her head flirtatiously and the earrings danced, catching the light and making the delicate strands shimmer in a way that was bewitching.

'They are gorgeous,' murmured Mrs Unwin, enthralled by the earrings. 'Where did you find something so… so unusual?'

'I bought them at the Arts and Craft Fair…' began Flora, but Henry grabbed her by the arm, steering her away to a corner.

'Sorry, I've just got to have a word with Flora,' Henry said over his shoulder to the Unwins.

Flora pulled herself free and glowered back at him. 'It has got nothing to do with you what I wear.'

'Yes, it has.' They were out of earshot but, keeping his voice under control, Henry went on, 'I know you didn't believe a word I told you the other day, but you are crazy, mad to show those earrings. We are being watched, you know, the whole time.'

Flora made a face at Henry.

'You'll see,' said Henry, 'and then you'll have to take me more seriously.'

Flora pushed past him, making for some other guests on the far side of the room.

Henry found Tom. 'Where is the loo?' he asked.

'You had better be quick, we're just about to sit down. It's back through the reception and then upstairs.'

Henry left the alcove where the party was gathered and headed back to the reception, passing several tables on his way. He nodded to the young couple at their table whom he had seen in reception when he arrived. He also noticed, which he thought was odd, a single diner sitting away from the other tables. It wasn't possible to see who it was because the person's face was hidden behind a newspaper. But whoever it was had horrible, long bony fingers.

On Henry's return to the restaurant his thoughts were firmly on the food he was about to enjoy. He was so engrossed in getting back to the party that he looked straight through the person sitting alone, the newspaper now neatly folded on the table.

Friendly calls directed Henry to his place between Flora and Tom, and he settled himself down.

Then he froze. In his mind he had seen the face belonging to the single diner a thousand times. The person sitting on her own was Mrs Wergs.

'Are you alright? You look as white as sheet.' Flora was concerned, and tried to feel Henry's forehead as if he had a temperature.

'Yes, I'm fine,' whispered Henry for no reason other than that his brain was whirling. 'Do you remember I was telling you about the woman I went to see in Craven Arms who told me all about your earrings?

That's her, sitting over there.' Henry nodded his head in the direction of Mrs Wergs' table. 'And she is not a human, she is really a goblin,' he added to drive his point home.

Flora had to crane her neck to the left. 'There's nobody sitting there, the table is empty. Henry, you should see a doctor.' Flora laughed.

Henry stood up, unable to believe that Mrs Wergs had vanished. 'She was right there, I promise. Not that you are going to believe me now, I know,' he said quietly.

'What are you two going on about?' joined in Tom, leaning across Henry to look at Flora.

'Henry thinks he has just seen a gob… Oww,' cried Flora, half-giggling as Henry stamped on her foot. Several guests looked over at them, wondering what the joke was all about.

'Those two never stop,' said Milly between mouthfuls.

The rest of the dinner went without a hitch. Everyone agreed the food surpassed all expectations. As the guests reluctantly began to leave, gathering coats and searching for car keys, Flora said she had to go to the loo. Tom repeated the directions and she disappeared upstairs.

Tom's mother went off to thank Claude while Tom and Henry dumped themselves in the armchairs by the bar to wait for Flora. After five minutes Tom thought Flora was taking too long. After ten he said he was going to go and check up on her. Just then Flora appeared, sobbing and looking upset.

'What's happened to you?' said Tom, alarmed.

'A woman, upstairs… attacked me!' Flora sat down on the arm of one of the armchairs. Drying her eyes and regaining some composure, she went on with an edge of anger to her voice, 'She tried to grab my earrings.'

For the second time that night Henry's mind was momentarily immobilised as he tried to take in what Flora had said. 'Mrs Wergs,' he mumbled.

Saying the words galvanised him into action, and he was out of the door and up the stairs, but despite a rapid search there was no sign of Mrs Wergs.

*

As they walked home up Corve Street, Flora's incident with Mrs Wergs was soon forgotten. Tom had his mother on his arm and Flora walked closely with Henry. The talk was all about the different courses, the red wine and funny stories worth repeating.

As they approached the Butter Cross they bumped into some of Tom and Henry's friends just about to go into the Church Inn before last orders.

'Come on, have a drink, we're just going to have a quick one.'

The group was persuasive and Milly helped by saying, 'Go on, all of you, don't worry about me, I'll be fine.'

Full of people, the bar was noisy and warm. But after their first drink Flora said she was tired and she was off home. Henry and Tom didn't argue and with Flora said their goodbyes. Outside the pub it was raining. As they stood for a moment, Flora suddenly said that she wanted to show the boys a picture in the window of Mr Bebb's art gallery.

'It's just round the corner.' She smiled.

'But it's raining,' said Tom.

'Just a quick look. I don't know why but I have fallen in love with this picture,' said Flora happily.

They turned right and walked into Church Street, the little alleyway that leads to the Market Square. Reaching the gallery, they all pressed their faces against the window, looking at the little Italian landscape painting.

'How much is it?' asked Tom, but before he got an answer, Flora, with a hint of alarm, said, 'What's that awful smell?'

'I can't smell a thing,' said Tom.

Henry looked round. At first he too couldn't smell anything. But in a moment it came to him as well.

Henry knew immediately. It was the unmistakable smell of goblin.

'Quick,' shouted Henry; the urgency in his voice shook the other two. But without waiting for their reaction, Henry pushed them both round the corner into a side alley that leads back towards the Butter Cross.

Flora screamed.

Henry, with his hands still on Tom and Flora, instinctively pulled them both back. Looking over Tom's shoulder, Henry saw a small dark figure squatting in the corner. In response to Flora's scream the figure sprang forward, its yellow eyes blazing, its goblin stench invading the air around them.

The goblin lunged at Flora, making her earrings a target for the second time that night. Henry, anticipating the goblins' move, twisted Flora out of the way, putting himself directly in the line of attack. Tom, dazed for a second by the speed of the attack, now came to Henry's help. The goblin's long arms were halfway to Henry's throat when Tom kicked the goblin's legs from under him, sending the creature sprawling on the wet pavement. Without a second thought Henry grabbed the stunned goblin by its long oily hair and banged its head hard on the pavement. There was a sickening groan and then silence.

'Follow me,' gasped Tom. Blindly following Tom, the three ran back the way they had come from the Church Inn. Behind the Butter Cross, Tom changed direction, turning left in College Street towards the alms houses and then right down past the door of St Laurence's Church. Following the path round the church they at last stopped outside its eastern end to catch their breath and listen for any pursuit.

The only noise was their panting breath and the drip of rainwater as it overflowed from a blocked gutter.

Tom pulled them back into the shadows of a porch, all their senses alert to danger. The rain was now falling steadily, partly obscuring the view across the graveyard and church green. Flora shivered with a mixture of cold and fear, and tucked herself between Tom and Henry. The veil of rain tinged with the orange light from the street lamps gave the silhouetted tombstones a life of their own. Their eyes played tricks as they strained to watch for another attack. Several times Flora softly cried, 'There,' but each time there was nothing.

'Just up a bit there is the passageway that leads into the courtyard behind the Bull Hotel,' said Henry in a whisper. 'Once through there we can turn right, run down Old Street and then cut across back to Broad Street.'

'OK,' said Tom, 'we all go together, you first, Henry, let's—'

But before he could finish his instructions Flora let out a whimper. Henry saw them too: several small dark figures had crawled like beetles over the parapet wall that runs the length of the church green. For a moment they crouched against the parapet then bending low, scuttled into the graveyard.

Flora was visibly shaking and began to quietly sob.

'They will see us if we move,' said Henry, shaking his head at Tom. A dog barked and from the direction of the church a man appeared. The Labrador was biting and tugging at its own lead despite the man's attempt to make the dog walk to heel.

Over the porch of the house beside which they were sheltering was an old wisteria. Its densely woven stems were flourishing but some parts were long dead. Tom grasped a section which was dry and brittle, and with a sharp tug freed a stick about a foot long.

Waiting for his moment, Tom stepped out of the shadows and waved the stick at the dog.

'Here, go fetch, here,' Tom shouted, and whistled until he had the dog's attention.

'Oi… hey… what are you doing? Don't be so stupid,' the man shouted angrily. But by now the dog had a mind of its own. Tom gave the stick one more wave in front of the dog and, with a well-judged throw, hurled the stick into the middle of the graveyard. The Labrador sprang forward, pulling its lead from the man's hand, and headed after the stick, barking with excitement.

'Come here, Poppy… what the hell do you think you are playing at?' snapped the man as he ran past Tom.

'Let's go,' said Tom. Even Flora managed a grin as Tom and Henry stifled a laugh as they watched man and dog disappearing in the direction of the goblins.

The three splashed their way home through the puddles, making nervous glances over their shoulders every other step, but without another sign of goblins they reached the front door of number 44.

Once in the kitchen Tom put the kettle on. 'OK, first thing, I will make us all a cup of coffee, then we need an explanation, Henry,' said Tom.

'The first thing I'm doing,' said Flora, 'is getting out of my wet clothes.'

A few minutes later Henry and Flora were sitting at the kitchen table in a mixture of dressing gowns and jerseys.

'Tom will be here in a second.' Flora yawned. 'I'm sorry, Henry, who would have believed your story? Up until tonight, I thought you had gone mad.'

Chapter 14

It wasn't until the following evening that Henry caught up with Tom and Flora. The three of them were slumped watching the television in the study. Tom was fidgety and a distraction to the other two as they tried to watch a programme.

'For heaven's sake, Tom,' Flora finally exploded, 'whatever's the matter with you?'

'OK, OK, it's just, I can't get Henry's story out of my mind. I keep telling myself it's ridiculous but then—'

'You saw them with your own eyes,' Flora interrupted him. 'What are you disputing? All three of us saw those vile things by the church, not to mention the attack on me by the gallery!'

Tom looked across at Henry for support. But Henry was deliberately trying to keep out of the conversation. The previous evening he hadn't finished telling his story until two in the morning. When he had finished Tom and Flora had stumbled off to bed, too dumbfounded to say anything. This was the first time they had talked about it.

'I cannot dispute the attack, but what was it? Are you really telling me that it was a goblin? That is something out of a book or a film, not here in Ludlow. And then there is this other country Henry just happens to walk into. He says it's full of elves looking for their king, who happens to be in Ludlow as well!' As Tom spoke he was still looking hard at Henry.

'I know it is hard to believe,' said Henry, getting up, 'but why should I make it up? I only managed to get into the "other country" because I was wearing the flute given to me by Owain or Min's sister, the girl who died.'

'What flute?' said Tom. 'You never mentioned a flute before.'

Henry hadn't said anything about the flute the previous night. He thought it would be safer if he kept it to himself.

'I know… but… OK. This is it.' Henry pulled the flute over his head from around his neck and laid it in the palm of his hand.

Flora got up to look more closely. 'It's beautiful… the carvings, I wonder if the same person who made my earrings also made your flute?'

'I never thought of that,' Henry reflected.

'Pass it over.' Tom beckoned with a wave of his hand.

Henry suddenly got cold feet about sharing his flute. He shook his head. 'I mustn't let it out of my sight,' which wasn't true. He was worrying what might happen to it, particularly if either of them tried to play it.

'Don't be ridiculous, I am not going to do anything with it. I just want to have a look,' said Tom with an edge to his voice.

Henry reluctantly passed the little instrument across to Tom, at the same time saying, 'Don't try to play it, please.'

'Why not?' said Tom, putting it to his lips.

'Don't think about it.' Henry dived across towards Tom. It was too late. With a short laugh, Tom blew on the flute.

'What's all the fuss, it's useless! It doesn't play a note.' Tom laughed again.

He was just about to try it once more when the lights went out and the television died. A draught crept into the room from under the French windows, making Flora shiver. The fire, which had been smouldering in the grate, reared up, spitting sparks onto the carpet. To everyone's alarm the wind began to gather strength. It rattled the windows, suddenly forcing them to burst open, allowing the cold air to rush in, flinging newspaper in all directions. Then on the wind came the sound of galloping horses. And with the horses came the noises of men going into battle. The thunder of hooves were mixed with the clatter of harnesses and the sharp ring of sword on sword. Over the swelling roar, spine-chilling war cries could be heard as the battle tempo increased. And above all the commotion there was one voice that could be clearly heard above all else. He was leading, rallying his troops, and guiding them forward.

It was too much for Flora. White as a sheet, she collapsed to the floor in a dead faint.

Tom and Henry were motionless, unable to respond and overwhelmed by the violent sounds filling the room. Then something snapped Henry out of the spell. He wrestled the flute out of Tom's hand. In a desperate measure, he too put the magic instrument to his lips. There was still no sound.

But miraculously, as if a knife had cut through the air, the noise and wind vanished.

Tom got to Flora first. 'Give me a hand, Henry,' he asked urgently.

Between them they picked her up and laid her on the sofa. Henry disappeared to the kitchen to get some water, but by the time he returned she was sitting up. Some colour had returned to her cheeks and she took a sip of water.

'Whose voice was that?' Flora looked worried. 'The man's voice… louder than anything else, we all heard him. You know, Henry, you know, don't you?'

'That was Owain,' answered Henry with a grin.

'Who?' checked Tom.

'Owain… Min, Tom, it was Min. That was some sort of message. What it means I am not sure. But it's make-your-mind-up time. Are you going to believe me now? I do need your help… please?'

'I don't think I have much choice, do I?' Tom said

as he started to tidy up the room by picking up the scattered pieces of newspaper.

*

The next day at breakfast, conversation around the table was limited to the odd grunt and lots of yawning when Flora suddenly said, 'I hear that there is a new girl working in the Deli on the Square.'

'Yes, I've heard that too,' joined in Milly, who was washing up, 'and she is very pretty apparently.'

'You had better go and have a look, boys.' Flora smirked, passing some plates to her mother.

'Actually,' Milly was now standing with the fridge door open, 'I do need some more cheese for tonight, could someone go to the deli for me? You can put it on the account.'

There was a brief silence as Tom and Henry looked at each other.

'I could do it after work,' said Henry. 'What type of cheese would you like?'

'Oh… you choose, anything you like.'

Tom leant across the table to Henry and tapped his nose. 'Full report tonight… OK?'

*

The morning in Bensons was uneventful, but the time slipped by. Henry became engrossed in mending a clock. In recent weeks Mr Benson had given him more repairs to carry out. With some help now and again, he was competent enough to dismantle a mechanism to find the problem. It was harder putting one back together, but he was getting better.

At twelve thirty Henry tidied up and put his coat on. There was a biting wind that morning.

'Bye, Henry, well done this morning.' Mr Benson seemed uncertain and was shuffling paper round his desk. 'Before you go,' Mr Benson found his diary, 'could you work morning and afternoon tomorrow? I don't know why, but we have got more work than ever.'

'OK, no problem.' Henry thought he could do with the extra money for his trip to Australia, and in any case he was enjoying his work.

Walking up Church Street, Henry paused outside Bebb's Gallery to look at the picture that Flora liked so much. It wasn't in the window, which probably meant somebody had bought it. *She will be sad*, he thought. As he stood by the gallery it was hard to imagine what had happened there several days ago.

He peered round the corner at the place the goblin had first lunged at Flora. He half expected to see some evidence of the attack, but the alleyway looked innocent enough.

Feeling the wind, he pulled the collar of his coat up round his ears and continued on towards the Market Square. Climbing the steps to the Deli on the Square,

Henry pushed the door open and the doorbell made its familiar ring.

Henry loved going into the deli. Each time he stepped inside there was the same slightly meaty, spicy smell and the friendly smiles of Maggie and Tracy. It was a small shop with two big counters selling every kind of cheese imaginable. Alongside the cheeses were delicious-looking meats and other tasty morsels. To make matters worse the shelves round the walls were piled with exotic bottles, neat packages and smart tins, all containing tempting food of one sort or another. It was almost impossible to come into the shop and leave without buying something that wasn't on your list.

Whilst the customers in front of him were being served, Henry enjoyed inspecting the shelves and choosing what he would buy if he had the money. He also looked to see if there was any sign of the new girl. It seemed only Maggie and Tracy were in the shop.

'Morning, Henry.' Maggie smiled. 'What would you like?'

'Hi, Maggie… I'm on an errand to buy some cheese. It's my choice… any suggestions?' Before Maggie could give Henry any advice there was the sound of somebody coming down the stairs from the storerooms.

'Henry, you haven't met Lexi before, have you?'

Henry turned to see a girl standing at the bottom of the stairs holding a tray of small round fruitcakes.

The girl was simply dressed, of medium height with shoulder-length hair. Her fair hair had a twist of red and lay on her shoulders in a rich swirl. There was a trace of freckles and her nose had a perfect line. Her eyes were playful, teasing Henry as he held her gaze.

In the split second that he took the girl in, there was something about her he couldn't quite fathom. That aside, he was entranced.

'No, we haven't. Hi… I'm Henry,' holding his hand out, which added an awkwardness to the moment.

'My hands are a bit full.' Lexi laughed as she laid the tray of cakes on top of the counter.

Just then the doorbell pinged again and several more customers came into the shop.

'Lexi, will you serve Henry?' said Maggie as she turned towards the new customers.

'He wants some cheese. Help him choose… let me know what it costs and it can go down in their account,' added Tracy.

Lexi slipped behind the counter, at the same time putting on an apron. 'I really don't know much about cheese, but this one here is popular, I think?' Lexi pointed at a large piece of hard-looking cheese.

'How much would you like?'

Henry was struggling. This was an altogether new experience. And it had caught him completely off balance. Henry would have bought a lump of coal if Lexi had told him to.

Lexi assumed that the cheese was fine since he hadn't commented on her choice. She cut and weighed it then wrapped it before passing it over to Henry.

'Thanks.' Henry smiled, taking the package. 'It'll be excellent, bye.'

'Bye, see you later,' called Lexi after Henry as he disappeared in a hurry out of the door.

Outside the deli, Henry paused to take a breath and to sort out his mind. He felt cross. He was sure he had just made a fool of himself. But at the same time he felt the raw exhilaration of the moment running through him. He had almost forgotten the cheese he was holding. He wondered, as he turned over the package wrapped in the deli's distinctive blue paper, how long it would take to eat such a huge chunk of cheese.

On the bottom of the package was some scrawled writing. At first he thought it was the cheese's name or the price. Looking more closely it said, 'Meet me in Ego's at one, Lexi.'

It took a second or two for the message to sink in. He checked his watch. It was just before a quarter to one. It was going to be a long fifteen minutes. He walked over to the market and wandered between the stalls. He was floating, a strange feeling of anticipation simmering inside him. Then unable to wait any more, Henry walked back to the archway into Quality Square. He crossed the little cobbled courtyard and pulled open the double doors of Ego's.

A seamless mix of coffee shop, wine bar and restaurant, Ego's was always full of activity. For locals, it was a habitual rendezvous and somehow a lot of others seemed to find their way there too. The decor was a shrine to Hollywood: photographs, many signed, and other movie memorabilia covered the walls.

As he expected the place was full. Pushing his way to the bar, he managed to catch Pierre's eye.

'A moment,' said Pierre as he started to make another batch of cappuccinos on the big Italian coffee machine.

'They're just leaving.' He indicated with his head in the direction of a tall table in the corner of the bar. A couple were draining their cups and gathering their shopping. As they struggled off through the crowd of drinkers by the bar, Henry slipped into their place, putting his coat over the other stool. It was the perfect position. Through the window, he had a view out over the cobbles to the archway and would be able to spot Lexi as she came into the courtyard.

Within a minute Pierre put a cappuccino in front of Henry. 'Another one when she arrives?' said Pierre, raising his eyebrows.

'OK.' Henry nodded. *Only a Frenchman*, he thought to himself, *would know that I'm waiting for a girl.*

Henry took a sip of his coffee and gazed out of the window, watching the first drops of rain slide down the glass.

Lexi appeared in the archway. She neatly sidestepped the fresh puddles and with a skip and a hop she was pulling at the door of Ego's. Henry, fascinated, watched her shake her head, running her fingers through her damp hair. Pulling her coat off, she caught him watching her.

'You found my scrawl. I was worried you might not see it.' She was slightly breathless but smiled, adding, 'It is so nice in here, isn't it?'

'What would you have done if I had not seen it?' said Henry, intrigued.

'I would have... found another way.' Pierre put down her cappuccino in front of her, breaking her line of thought. 'What is this?' Lexi was puzzled.

'It's coffee, silly,' answered Henry. 'I thought you might need a good cappuccino after a morning in the deli. How long have you worked there? Not long?'

Lexi took a careful taste of her coffee. She wrinkled her nose and pulled a face. 'What a strange taste!' and she pushed the cup and saucer away.

'Hey... they make the best cappuccinos here.' Henry looked wounded but quickly recovered. 'Have something else?'

'Can I have a glass of water? I would just love some water.' Lexi settled herself more comfortably on the stool, staring back at Henry with her pale blue eyes.

'How long have you been in Ludlow?' Henry motioned to Pierre for a glass of water. 'Where do you live... close by?' Henry kept talking as Pierre passed a tall tumbler of iced water across the bar.

‘Have we met before? Where were you at school?’ Henry was now desperate to find something they had in common.

‘Henry,’ said Lexi quietly. ‘Henry—’

‘I know. You were working in—’ continued Henry before Lexi put her hand on his arm.

‘Henry, listen to me. We have never met before.’

As they looked at each other, awkwardness returned to Henry. ‘I’m sorry… I was sure…’

‘Henry,’ Lexi leant forward, ‘Owain sent me.’

‘Owain, Min?’ Henry leant closer. ‘You’re from Min, that’s impossible.’

‘Why?’ Lexi looked serious.

‘If Min sent you… you’re an elf.’ The words sounded stupid and Henry looked around, worried that he had been overhead.

‘Of course I am. Min sent me to help you find our king. He told you he was sending someone when you came to Gwynedd.’ Lexi was no longer keeping her voice down and several people at the bar looked at them at the mention of the word ‘king’.

‘Shhhh… were you there? I never saw you in the tree village.’

‘I saw you. I listened to your story. I was in the shadows, when everyone was gathered round the fire. I heard how you found the book, about your kidnap by the goblins and how you were nearly eaten by cannibals before you escaped.’

Henry looked across at the perfect girl opposite

him. Was it possible that she was sent by Min and was… an elf? He reached inside his shirt, pulling out the little flute from around his neck, and held it up in front of Lexi.

Without a word, Lexi put her hands round her neck and pulled a thin chain over her head. On the chain was another flute. As she held it up next to Henry's flute, he could see it was identical.

*

They left Ego's in the drizzling rain.

Under the arch, Lexi touched Henry's arm. 'Come, I want you to meet a friend.'

As they turned down Church Street Henry stopped. 'You've never had a cappuccino before, have you?'

Lexi, without stopping or turning her head, said, 'No, never!'

Henry caught up with her and started laughing. 'That's better proof than a flute.'

They reached the corner of Church Street and College Street. A beggar was sitting on a pile of dirty old rugs with his long legs drawn up close to his chin. In his hands was a penny whistle on which he was playing an almost inaudible tune. Sharing the man's rugs was a scraggy lurcher and in front of them was a cap strewn with a few coins. Henry had passed him a hundred times, hardly noticing him.

'Henry, meet Lazy Jack. He is one of us. And this is

his dog, Sugar.' Lexi bent forward and scratched Sugar behind his ear.

Lazy Jack didn't move but looked up at them both, then winked in Henry's direction.

'Nothing happens on these streets without me knowing about it.' His voice was quiet but gruff and Henry had to stoop to hear him more clearly.

'So, what is the latest?' asked Lexi, who crouched down next to Lazy Jack.

'Don't hang about here, they're everywhere. They know you're here. Keep walking.' Lazy Jack started to play his whistle again. Sugar got up, stretching and wagging his tail.

Lexi stood up. 'Thanks, I know we've got to be careful.'

'Something for the dog?' called Lazy Jack to no one in particular.

Henry dropped some change into the shabby cap then Lexi and Henry turned to retrace their steps up Church Street.

As they passed the greengrocer's stalls laid out on the street, Lexi paused, looking at the neatly displayed fruit and vegetables. She picked up a large orange. 'Henry, what is this?' Her voice was full of awe as she turned the fruit over in her hand.

Henry was about to say that she was having him on when he realised that she might really never have seen an orange before.

'It's an orange, it's delicious. Here, you can have it.'

Henry reached in his pocket and paid the lady standing by the stall. With an irrepressible smile, Lexi carried the orange like an orb back to the deli.

Outside the steps to the deli, Lexi paused. 'I have got to introduce you to more friends. I will get a message to you.'

'But what about the plan to find the king? What are we going to do?' asked Henry with a touch of impatience.

'The plan… is well in hand,' replied Lexi as she pushed open the door which made its distinctive ring.

'You don't know how to eat that orange, do you?' Henry looked up at her from the pavement.

'I'm not going to eat it, it's far too precious! Bye, see you later,' and she was gone.

Chapter 15

Henry managed to avoid seeing Tom until the following evening. He couldn't stop thinking about Lexi. It was hard enough working out his own feelings, let alone trying to tell Tom about her.

He was the last to come in and sit down at the table for supper. Tom waited for him to get his food then asked, 'Well…?'

'Well… what?' Henry knew perfectly well what Tom meant.

'What was she like?' Tom couldn't pretend to be serious for long and started to laugh. 'What is the new girl in the deli like?'

Milly and Flora put their knives and forks down to hear Henry's answer.

'Why is everyone so interested? It's no big deal,' said Henry, looking round at the expectant faces. He realised he wasn't going to get away with saying nothing. 'OK… OK, yes… like you said, she is gorgeous!'

'And?' said Flora.

'And?' Henry looked surprised.

'And,' went on Flora, 'you had a cup of coffee with her in Ego's!'

Tom leant backwards, balancing his chair on two legs. 'I'm impressed, you don't hang about, do you!'

'I was only… being kind, she, Lexi, is new to Ludlow and I thought it would be good to show her around. In any case, how did you know that?'

Flora gave Henry an irritating grin and said nothing.

The business of eating supper resumed. Silence settled over the table as they contemplated their food.

*

After supper was cleared away, Henry waited until Tom's mother had disappeared into her office.

Flora got up, stretched and headed for the kitchen door too.

'Just before you go, I need to tell you a bit more about Lexi.' Henry was talking to Flora, but he turned to Tom, who was now flicking through the *Ludlow Journal*.

Tom grinned. 'Mmm… go on then.'

'I know you thought I was quick off the mark. She actually asked to see me.'

Flora had the kitchen door half open, but she closed it, leaning her back on the door. 'So…' she said, intrigued.

‘So,’ went on Henry, ‘when we had a cup of coffee in Ego’s she told me…’ he paused to allow his next words to carry more weight, ‘she told me she had been sent by Owain, Min. She was here to help us find the elf king.’

Flora gasped, putting her hand across her mouth. ‘I don’t believe it!’

Tom folded the paper into a baton and banged the table. ‘Yeah… nor do I. How do you know? Can she prove it?’

‘She can actually,’ said Henry triumphantly. ‘She has around her neck exactly the same little flute that I showed you the other day with dramatic consequences… remember?’ Henry snatched the rolled-up paper from Tom and playfully hit him over the head.

‘Stop it, you two.’ Flora moved between them. ‘When can we meet her? A real elf. I still cannot believe it!’

‘I am sure you can.’ Henry felt he was in control. ‘When I see her next, I will ask her back here to meet you… to meet you both. OK, Tom?’ Henry clapped Tom on the back and followed Flora out of the kitchen, in the direction of the television.

*

Over the following weeks Henry and Lexi met regularly. He took her home as promised and introduced her to Tom and Flora.

During that first meeting Lexi talked about Gwydden: the forests that reached as far as the eye could see, swimming and picnics by rivers with crystal-clear pools, her people and their strange villages up in the trees. But above all they liked hearing about the gold that came from the Black Mountains. Talk of gold brought the subject round to goblins and the goblin wars that had wreaked such devastation on the elfish people.

'That is why we need to find our king so badly,' Lexi said. 'Only with him at the head of the elfish army can we start to recover the land that we have lost, the gold mines and, last but not least, our dignity as a nation.' She paused to watch their faces.

'But there is worse to tell you. The goblins know about the elf king. They know that he is somewhere in Ludlow. And of course they know about Henry, and as Lazy Jack said, they probably know about me.

'But like us they have got to track him down. It is a race against time. If they find him first, they will kill him. And then any hope of winning back everything that we have lost will be gone… forever!'

'So what is the plan then? How are we going to find him?' Tom was hooked by Lexi's stories. Gone was the note of scepticism in his voice.

'We do have one advantage over the goblins. Well, two actually.' Lexi reached into her shirt and pulled out the flute hanging round her neck. Putting it to her lips, she made it look as if she was playing a tune.

‘There’s no sound, you cannot hear a note. Henry’s is exactly the same.’ As he talked, Tom got up and started to walk round the table. ‘What is the point of it if you cannot hear it?’

‘You’re not meant to hear anything,’ Lexi said quietly but with a hint of steel they hadn’t heard before. She continued, ‘The pair of flutes were made long before the death of King Cleddau. They were made by the descendant of the same craftsman who made the earrings for Nior’s fateful wedding. Their magic is legend. Their powers are a mystery but one story about them has never been disputed.’

Flora madly prodded Henry to make her point that she had guessed their origin. Now she couldn’t help but interrupt. ‘Are my earrings magic as well?’

‘Flora, do shut up. Let Lexi finish.’ Tom and Henry almost spoke together, desperate for her to finish.

‘Yes. I suppose they could be… but…’ Lexi smiled, ‘but the only person who can hear the flute is the rightful heir to the elfish crown, that is, the king himself!’

*

It was more than cold that November. The wind flew in from the east, cutting under doors and slicing through coats. The townsfolk of Ludlow, well wrapped up, went about their business crouched against the painful wind. The hard, frosty pavements were not the place to pass the time of day. In preference they hurried home to their fires rather than linger on street corners.

After their first meeting with Lexi, Henry, Tom and Flora promised to help her with the search. But Henry and Lexi were the only two who showed real enthusiasm for the job.

They began their search by exploring every corner of the town. They bought a map of Ludlow and divided it into sections. With military planning they covered every street, all the pubs, and each fish and chip shop. They included bus stops, the market and visited schools as the children came out at the end of their day. They stepped in and out of every shop, watched whatever film was showing at the Assembly Rooms in Mill Street. And they even went to watch Ludlow United play at home. At each place they visited, they would, without drawing attention to it, play the little flute.

The days merged into weeks and all the while the cold persisted. Each foray into Ludlow was a contest with the elements. But somehow the spirit of their quest overcame the numbness in their fingers and toes. And Henry began to depend on their time together.

But with nothing to show for all their hard work, frustration was beginning to creep in.

*

'How are you getting on?' asked Tom as he and Henry rode out from Downton stables early one Saturday morning.

'Not very well. And thanks for your help. I thought you were going to lend a hand?' Henry's tone was more disappointed than anything else.

'I want to help, I know I said I would. But we cannot walk about as a gang. Flora wouldn't want to miss out, so that would be four of us trooping round looking for a king!' Pausing, Tom lifted his left leg to tighten the girth. 'The other point is that there are only two flutes—'

'OK, OK I get the point. I agree, we cannot go on like this, peering into every shop, pub or anywhere else. People will start talking, if they haven't already.'

'I've got an idea,' said Tom as he eased his horse into a canter.

Henry kicked his horse into a canter too, but it wasn't until the far end of the gallops that they caught up with each other. Their horses were steaming from the exertion of their impromptu race. While catching his breath, Henry took his feet from the stirrups and leant forward, putting his arms around his horse's neck.

'What's your big idea then?' he asked as he sat up and moved his horse closer to Tom.

'Remember telling us about Lazy Jack? You also mentioned that Lexi had said there were other "friends" in Ludlow. Why don't we ask Lexi to get them all together and have a sort of… well, a conference? A meeting to discuss how to get the job done.'

'I'll ask her. I am seeing her later.' Henry turned his horse back towards the stables. 'Let's walk back, no galloping. In any case we are being watched by the boss.' Henry nodded in the direction of a four-wheel drive car perched on the top of the hill about half a mile away. It wasn't difficult to make out the profile of the trainer as he watched them through binoculars.

*

As they had planned, Henry met Lexi outside the bakers on the Market Square just after one o'clock.

'Will you buy me a hot pie?' she asked.

They stamped their feet to keep warm as they quickly ate their pies outside the shop.

'Lexi,' Henry picked his moment, 'when I was riding out with Tom this morning I had a go at him for not helping us. Well not "a go", just a dig, really.'

'Well done,' said Lexi with her mouth full.

'But he was right, we need to do something new, a change of plan. What we have been doing is great, but it hasn't produced anything.' Henry looked closely at her for a reaction.

'When we have finished I will introduce you to Roger.' Lexi sounded matter-of-fact.

'Is he an elf too?' joked Henry.

'Don't mock. Of course he is.' Lexi gave Henry a hard stare and went on, 'Actually, he is the most important elf in Ludlow.'

'Are there lots of your people in Ludlow? Are there… elves everywhere?' Henry was serious.

But she ignored his question. 'Right, are you finished?' She gave Henry her scrunched-up paper bag and set off in the direction of Mill Street. Henry found a bin and hurried after her.

Turning the corner into Mill Street, she walked the short distance to Farmers and disappeared into the shop.

Farmers was a fruit and vegetable shop. It had one large airy room with a high ceiling and a doorway that was permanently open to the pavement. Around the walls and in the centre, in a disorganised display, were boxes and crates piled with fresh produce. Each box had a hand-scrawled note telling the shopper the origin of the contents and the price. The choice was almost limitless. On the left by the open door were knobbly pink fir apple potatoes from Herefordshire, fennel and broad beans from the Marches. And across the aisle there were winter strawberries, lychees and mangos from warmer climates. At intervals paper bags hung on a string loop. Locals moved briskly down between the boxes, snatching paper bags as they shopped, knowing exactly what they wanted and where it was. Visitors pondered, enjoying the choice and taking their time.

There weren't any tills. The staff, with mittened hands, pulled out scraps of cardboard and made rapid lists of figures in soft pencil. Purchases were stuffed into bags and maybe a pot of local honey or home-made biscuits added to the bag.

The shop was busy. Lexi sidestepped some browsing customers and disappeared behind a screen at the far end of the room. Henry hung back, waiting by the door. He busied himself by looking over the cut flowers and potted shrubs that were also part of the stock on sale.

After what seemed an age, she reappeared with a man that Henry assumed must be Roger.

Roger was medium height but walked with a slight stoop. His hair was his most distinctive feature. It was like a black woolly mop. *Similar to an old English sheepdog*, Henry thought to himself.

'Henry, this is Roger. Roger, Henry.' Lexi was brisk and the two men nodded to each other. She walked out of the shop, away from any customer who might be trying to eavesdrop, expecting Henry and Roger to follow her.

On the pavement and away from the shop entrance, Lexi went on, 'Roger is going to call a meeting. I have explained everything to him. But he knew it all anyway.'

'Get here say about eight tonight? Just come straight in. The door will be closed by then. Not locked, though.' Roger spoke very fast and with a strong accent that didn't seem quite local so Henry had to concentrate to understand.

But Lexi nodded, and with no more to discuss, Roger, with a salute to Henry, shuffled back to work.

*

Tom was pleased that his idea had been acted on.

With his coat on, Tom shouted up the stairs, 'Come on, Flora, you're going to make us late.'

The three of them walked up Broad Street and then left towards Market Square, where they met up with Lexi. She slipped her hand through Henry's arm. 'I'm so cold,' she said. 'Where have you been?'

Keeping an eye open for anyone suspicious following them, they pushed open the door of Farmers a little after eight. There were no lights on in the main part of the shop, but there was a faint glow from behind the screen that Lexi had earlier disappeared behind to find Roger. After locking the door, Lexi led the way down the aisles between the fruit and vegetables covered in a patchwork of dust sheets.

She peered round the screen, nearly bumping into Roger. The others followed; Roger guided each one with a touch on their arm towards a seat. The faint glow they had seen came from a single candle in a jam jar. The stacked boxes and crates stood out like stone columns and against the flickering light they threw tall spooky shadows across the high ceiling. The room was cold and had a musty smell like a potato store but mixed with the sweet smell of fruit. The earthy dust made Flora sneeze and she had to borrow Tom's handkerchief.

Henry made himself comfortable on a sack that turned out to be full of carrots. Flora and Tom were perched together on a crate of cabbages. There was just enough light for Henry to make out the shapes of a least a dozen other people seated in silence on the sacks between the columns of crates. As they settled themselves it was possible to see some of their faces. He recognised the antique dealer in Broad Street who also sold wine. There was a familiar face of a checkout lady from Tesco, and he wasn't sure but it looked like the man who owned the little beer shop in Lower Corve Street. In the corner, sitting on the floor, was Lazy Jack with Sugar, who looked up at Henry with expectant eyes. As he searched for other faces somebody blew out the candle.

For a few seconds the room was blacked out. Then a faint light, orange-tinged, crept in from the street lighting. Roger's voice broke the silence. He spoke in low tones, using his arms to illustrate his message. As he spoke there were whispers from the audience and Henry strained forward to understand what was being said. Then he realised that it wasn't any human tongue that was being used.

'What are they saying?' Flora whispered hoarsely in Henry's direction. 'I can't understand a word.'

'Nor can I. It must be elfish.' Henry got up and leant across Flora to whisper in Tom's ear, 'Where is Lexi?'

'No idea, she was here.'

As Tom answered, Lexi appeared from the shadows to stand alongside Roger. Roger gestured that it was her turn to speak and sat down by her side.

Lexi paused, looking round at her audience. Quietly, she began to address them. 'This is the first full Ludlow council meeting, on this side, for many, many years. The council meets all together only in extreme cases. Roger has described the situation to the councillors and heard their reports. The news is getting worse by the day. The truth is they have an army gathering, probably able to attack at any moment.'

Turning to Henry, Tom and Flora, she went on, 'Leading the army is Sla. We elves know him as "the bleak goblin". He is a direct descendant of Droch. His stronghold was originally in the north, but over the years his power spread and now extends to all corners of the goblin empire. He is the most evil and ruthless goblin to walk the earth. His name "bleak" is well justified.'

There were mutterings from several of the shapes when Lexi mentioned Sla's name.

She went on, 'Sla has one final ambition. Not just content to rule the goblin world, he has to stamp out the elfish people once and for all. But now he also believes that the elfish royal line might not be dead, as had been thought. And he knows what danger that means.'

Lexi looked round again at the shadowy gathering.

Looking in the direction of one of the councillors she continued, 'A few councillors think the goblins already know where the king is. But the rest are not sure. However, we have to find him first. The councillors will now call upon all their people, all the elves on the human side, all their agents and contacts to trace and find the king. That will start immediately and we,' Lexi looked at Henry, Tom and Flora, 'must find other places, opportunities, anything to carry on searching. This weekend there is a medieval winter festival in the castle, which will be a good chance. But between now and then or even after, there is no rest until we have found him.'

As Lexi finished there was the sound of people outside on the pavement.

'The film has finished in the Assembly Rooms, nothing to worry about.' Henry's words took away a look of alarm on Flora's face.

Roger stood up, putting his arm round Lexi. In something elfish he spoke again and the meeting started to break up.

'What do we do?' asked Flora.

'Sit tight for a moment,' said Tom.

Henry nodded in agreement as he joined them on their crate of cabbages.

A few feet from them, Roger started to move a pallet half piled with Brussel sprouts in red net sacks. He finished the job with a good shove with his boot.

After scratching around on the floor he pulled up a trap door.

Lexi moved across to her friends. 'There is an underground passage leading from here. Roger thinks it would be sensible for the councillors to use it. We will go out the front door and mingle with the people leaving the film.'

In silence, the councillors stepped down through the trap door and one by one disappeared. Roger closed the door and pushed the pallet back to its original place. He brushed the dust off his shirt and reached inside his pocket, pulling out a bunch of keys.

'Ready, let's go.' Lexi was keen to go and the others followed her back to the front door. Outside filmgoers were still spilling onto the pavement. The four joined in the crowd and without a backward glance left Roger to lock up.

Passing through the crowd, the four regrouped on the other side of Mill Street.

'I'm starving,' said Tom, 'I need something to eat.'

The others agreed and they were about to set off when a noisy group of drinkers tumbled out of the Blue Boar. Half a dozen men milled about in a drunken gaggle, shouting and laughing. In a moment they blocked the pavement. Tom took the lead and with the girls close behind him they skirted round the rowdy gang. Henry followed close behind.

From the middle of the group stepped a figure that Henry recognised from his first day at Bensons. He was the gang leader outside the shop and the troublemaker up in court for fighting that had been reported, as Tom had spotted, in the *Ludlow Journal*.

'You're just my sort.' The youth made a lunge at Lexi, grabbing her scarf and pulling her backwards.

Coming up behind them, Henry didn't hesitate. He threw his arm around the neck of Lexi's assailant, attempting to pull him off her and bring him to the ground. But his target was a big lad with broad shoulders and he shrugged off Henry's first attempt. Lexi had broken free, but Henry was still convinced that she was in danger. Before he could launch a second attempt, the youth turned and, with a drunken yell, charged at Henry, sending them both sprawling into the gutter.

By now the drunken mob was relishing the situation and goaded their leader on with wild cries of encouragement. The noise attracted unwelcome attention and in a minute a crowd began to gather.

The shouting only stopped when a police car pulled up by the figures writhing on the ground.

PC Roberts and PC Phillips didn't ask any questions. They hauled the two fighters to their feet, handcuffed them and, ducking their heads down, put them both into the back of the police car. Distraught, Lexi, Tom and Flora watched as the blue flashing light sped off down Mill Street in the direction of the police station.

*

Sergeant Royson was a formidable man. Standing six foot and four inches with 'prop forward' shoulders and hands like plates, he was a giant. His face was bright shiny pink and his head, save for a horseshoe ring of grey hair, was a polished dome. In an immaculate uniform showing three silver stripes on each arm, he towered over the duty desk, intimidating anybody visiting the station, for whatever reason.

But that night his normally stern face was decorated with a satisfied smile. The message on the radio from Roberts and Phillips had made his long shift a pleasure. This time he was going to make sure 'that lad' would go down for a long time. He might have got away lightly before. But street fighting again should guarantee a healthy spell behind bars. While he waited, he drummed his pencil on the blotter, savouring the moment.

From Mill Street it was a five-minute drive to the large, modern police station. On cue, Sergeant Royson heard the police car pull into the car park, the blue flashing light momentarily filling the duty room like a disco.

The swing doors banged open as PCs Roberts and Phillips elbowed their way through into the duty room, guiding their charges towards the desk.

'You can't keep away, can you? We could name a cell after you.' Sergeant Royson glowered at the person standing next to Henry. 'Take him away, I know his details off by heart.' Eying Henry up and down, he pointed his pencil at him, 'You stay there, my friend; I haven't seen you before.' The sergeant signalled to Henry to stay put as 'that lad' was taken to the cells.

After giving all the usual details to Sergeant Royson, Henry was taken to an interview room. The room was depressingly bare apart from two chairs and a table. After an age, PC Roberts appeared with a sheaf of paper and some pencils.

'Right, young man,' PC Roberts cleared his throat, 'time to make a statement. Write in your own words exactly what happened, OK?'

Henry looked at him, hoping for some words of comfort like, 'None of this is your fault and you will be out here in no time,' but the constable turned on his heels and disappeared, locking the door behind him.

It took about ten minutes for Henry to put everything down on the blank forms provided, but it was an hour before PC Roberts returned.

'Right, son, here's a cup of tea.' The policeman was friendlier this time. 'Sergeant Royson will be having a word with you.' *Perhaps*, thought Henry, *he knows what I'm in for and is feeling sorry for me.*

After another interminable wait, Henry picked up the sound of heavy feet coming down the corridor towards the door of the interview room.

Sergeant Royson walked as if he owned the place. He put a slim file on the table but didn't sit down.

Henry nearly yawned. It was late and he was suddenly very tired. Sensibly, he controlled his yawn and looked expectantly at the sergeant.

'I've read your statement.' Sergeant Royson sounded detached. 'We haven't made a decision on what to do with you yet, so you're stopping here. But you cannot stay in this room.' Picking up the file from the table, he made for the door. 'This way,' he said without turning round.

In the corridor he turned left and in a few paces stopped outside a cell door.

'We seem to have a full house tonight, don't know why? You will have to share. But don't start fighting again.' There was a clear threat in his voice. Henry felt he was a man not worth crossing. The heavy metal door with a peephole at eye level was swung open. After he stepped inside it crashed shut. The lock clunked behind him.

Inside the brightly lit cell there was a single built-in bench against the wall at the far end. Otherwise there was no other furniture. Huddled in the left-hand corner, with his legs drawn up under his chin, was the person responsible for this nightmare. Saying nothing, Henry took the opposite end of the bench. He was exhausted and drained by what had happened in such a short time. Slumping into the corner, he was thankful to close his eyes.

*

Henry woke in the small hours of the morning. He had fallen asleep in an awkward position and was now painfully stiff. He stretched his aching limbs. The figure in front of him didn't move.

Looking round his sparse cell, any thought of sleep had left him. A sense of déjà vu stole into his head. He almost smiled when he remembered his imprisonment by the goblins. The thoughts of his time underground and his escape took his mind on a dream, racing through all that had happened to him. He stopped when he thought of Lexi. Thinking of her brought back into sharp focus the meeting in Farmers and the urgency of the whole situation. How could he now be in this position, locked in a police cell with so much at stake?

Consoling himself he reached for his flute. Pulling it out from under his shirt, he started to play an imaginary tune to himself.

The figure at the other end of the bench stirred. Waking from a deep sleep, Henry's fellow prisoner stretched and sat up.

Henry kept playing the little flute.

'That's nice, that's really nice. I wish I could play like that.' His cellmate resumed his huddled position and went back to sleep.

Chapter 16

Henry looked across at the sleeping figure at the far end of the bench. All the stress of the last few hours slipped away. Unable to contain his excitement, he got up and started to pace about the little cell. He couldn't think straight. He had to try and put some order into his mind.

The body on the bench stirred. 'Can't you sit still?' it said grumpily.

'You wouldn't sit still if you knew what I knew.' Henry was fumbling to find the right thing to say.

'What do you mean?'

A thin strand of a plan filtered into Henry's mind. 'The sergeant on the desk told me that you could go down for a good few years.'

The body turned over to face the wall. 'I've heard that before,' he said pulling the sweatshirt hood over his head.

‘What would you say if I could get you out of here? Away from here. Away from getting into trouble the whole time. A clean break.’

‘Don’t be daft!’ came a muffled reply.

‘I’m serious.’ Henry had no idea what he was promising. ‘I really can get you out of here.’ There was no response. Henry sat down on the bench close to the huddled figure. ‘I don’t know your name. I’m Henry.’ There was a silence. ‘I can’t help you if I don’t know your name.’

After a long pause, the figure, without moving or turning round, said, ‘Will.’

*

The heavy footsteps of Sergeant Royson sounded down the corridor. After a jangle of keys the cell door was unlocked.

‘Right, you,’ Sergeant Royson pointed at Henry, ‘come with me. Say your goodbyes. You won’t be seeing him again… well, not for a long time.’ The sergeant laughed loudly and stood to one side to let Henry out.

‘We’re best friends now,’ said Will, suddenly getting off the bench and coming over to the door. ‘And he’s promised to get me out of here.’

Henry winced and Sergeant Royson burst out laughing again.

Back in the duty room, Sergeant Royson got behind his desk. ‘OK, young man, you’re free to go now. You are lucky this time, but let it be a lesson. Right, I don't want to see you again.' The sergeant put his head down into his paperwork, which was a signal for Henry to leave.

But Henry stood his ground. Sergeant Royson looked up when he realised that Henry wasn't leaving.

'Is there something I've missed?' growled the sergeant.

'No,' said Henry, 'no, not at all. But Will asked me if I could get him a change of clothes. I know his sister. Can she come down with some clean stuff?'

Sergeant Royson was taken aback for a moment. 'Yeah, OK, yeah… but no funny business, OK? What's her name?'

'Lexi. Thanks.' Henry was halfway to the door. 'I will get her to come down straight away.'

Henry ran all the way to the Market Square. He only stopped to catch his breath outside the deli. It was just before nine o'clock and Henry was hoping that Lexi would arrive for work at any moment.

Maggie popped her head out of the deli door. 'She's already here, do you want her? I hear you were very brave…'

Lexi pushed past Maggie, jumped down the steps and flung her arms around Henry.

'I will leave you two to it.' Maggie smiled, shaking her head as she disappeared back through the door.

'We've been beside ourselves! What's happened?' Lexi was bemused by Henry's broad smile. He should have been looking miserable!

He waited until Maggie had closed the shop door. 'Guess what? I've found him, I think I've found your lost king!' Henry's voice bubbled over with excitement.

'Found him? But you have been locked up in the police station all night. We tried to see you or speak to you; the police weren't at all helpful. What's been going on?'

'Ask Maggie if you can have half an hour… say it's really important.' Henry climbed the steps and pushed open the door. 'Quick, we haven't got much time.'

Lexi reappeared in a couple of seconds. 'She's fine, I'll take a shorter lunch break. What are we doing?'

Henry took Lexi by the arm. 'The first thing is to get some of my clothes… I will explain as we go.'

By the time they had got home and Henry had stuffed some clothes into a bag, he had explained to Lexi everything that had happened.

'I had to tell Will that we would get him out. I've no idea how, though,' Henry said, trying to get a reaction out of Lexi. She had been strangely quiet as she had listened to Henry's ordeal and the discovery of Will.

'Don't worry, the council have been planning this for years. Roger will know what to do… let's go.' Lexi spoke as if her mind was a million miles away.

In silence they headed back to the police station, cutting through Brand Lane and then up Old Street. They ran down Lower Galdeford, getting to the police station just after nine thirty.

Sergeant Royson looked up from his desk. 'I had hoped that I wasn't going to see you again,' he said, stifling a yawn. 'This way. Five minutes, that's all.' Pulling out his keys on a silver chain from his pocket, he led the way down to the cells. He unlocked the heavy door and walked into the cell. 'Look sharp, you've got visitors.'

Will was sitting hunched up in the same corner. He looked puzzled to see Henry again, if not confused about Lexi standing there as well.

'Your sister has got a change of clothes.' Sergeant Royson spat out the word 'sister' as if he didn't believe it. The doubt in his voice continued, 'How do I know he is your brother, anyway?'

Lexi stepped past the policeman and, taking the bag from Henry, handed it to Will. 'Because,' said Lexi without any hesitation, 'he has a pink birthmark on his left leg, by his kneecap.'

'Well, have you?' said the sergeant.

Will looked hard at Lexi then rolled up the left leg of his trousers. As Lexi had said, there was a pink birthmark by his knee.

'OK, OK, that's enough. Time's up.'

Lexi, ignoring the order, gave Will a hug. Startled, Will muttered a thanks for the clothes. 'I'm sorry about what happened… can you come again?' he asked a little sheepishly.

'What, and bring a cake with a key in it?' Sergeant roared with laughter at his joke. 'Not likely. Anyway, you're off to Shrewsbury nick tonight.' The sergeant pushed Henry and Lexi out of the cell. The door was slammed shut and locked, bringing the visit to an abrupt close.

As Sergeant Royson headed up the corridor, Lexi turned and, through the peephole, whispered, 'See you later.'

On the way back to the deli, Lexi stopped off at Farmers and spent a few minutes talking to Roger. Afterwards, Henry asked umpteen times about the plan, but all she would say was that it was all in Roger's hands.

*

Sergeant Royson finished his shift at five o'clock that evening. He was annoyed. Will was to be collected at six by the police from Shrewsbury. He wanted to be there to ensure that he really was leaving his patch, but he had made a long-standing promise to his wife to take her to the Ludlow pubs darts final in the Church Inn. It was a shame; his first pint that night would have been that much sweeter if he had dispatched 'that lad' off to Shrewsbury himself.

There was something else that niggled him. Sergeant Morrison, the duty sergeant he was handing over to that night, was now going to be late. He was picking his daughter up from hospital, dropping her home and then coming on to the station at about eight thirty. Until then, PC Phillips would be in charge. And he wasn't the brightest person, which was what worried Sergeant Royson.

As if to prove his point, Sergeant Royson had to go over the evening's procedures several time before he felt Phillips understood what he had to do. Even then he wasn't sure. He left just after five o'clock with a nervous ache in the pit of his stomach.

Phillips was relieved to see the back of Sergeant Royson. He was fussing over the simple matter of handing over a prisoner. It was something that he had done a hundred times.

He made himself a large pot of tea. After a second's thought he opened the cell to give Will a mug of tea as well. The lad seemed no trouble at all.

Sitting down at last, he was about to flick through the paper when the telephone rang. The caller was reporting a stolen bicycle and he dutifully took down all the details. As soon as he finished the call, the phone rang again. This time it was a suspected break-in. He was on his third call, about a domestic disturbance, when the antique dealer, from Broad Street (the one who sold wine), walked into the police station. He had come in to report another suspected burglary. In the space of ten minutes PC Phillips' world had gone mad.

As if things couldn't get worse, a contract cleaner with her assistant pushed through the door carrying buckets and mops. They both looked and dressed identically. Each had curly fair hair under a headscarf and was wearing overalls emblazoned with 'Sparkle Cleaning Services'. The older cleaner was a bossy, no-nonsense woman. The type of person it's not worth crossing.

'Evening, Officer.' She looked Phillips straight in the eye. 'We're the cleaners asked for earlier, I understand your regulars have let you down. We'll get started right away, shan't get in your way, sir.'

Phillips couldn't remember if Sergeant Royson had mentioned this or not. 'Have you got any ID? How many are you?'

Just then the antique dealer started to get agitated that he wasn't getting the right attention. 'Look here, Constable,' he said, 'I want you to take these details down now.' Phillips didn't know which way to turn. Tutting under her breath, the bossy cleaner held up an official-looking badge with one hand and with the other hand showed three figures.

'I can only see two of you,' muttered Phillips as he reached for a report form.

'She's in the van. Getting the Hoovers and things. We'll best be getting on.' The cleaner and her assistant, with their buckets and mops, passed through in the direction of the offices and the cells. While Phillips attended to the antiques dealer, the cleaners went about their business, coming and going in the background.

The report was nearly done when the assistant cleaner burst into the duty room. 'Sorry to interrupt, sirs, but there's somebody in one of the cells sounding very ill. You'd better come straight away.'

Phillips looked apologetically at the antique dealer. The dealer shrugged his shoulders. 'Better go,' he said helpfully.

Phillips hurried down the corridor, pulling out his keys. 'Right here,' pointed out both the cleaners. Phillips could hear the inmate retching.

'He needs the bathroom, and quick,' said the bossy cleaner, her hands on her hips, glaring at Phillips as he fumbled for the right key.

As he pulled the cell door open, Phillips had to catch Will as he tumbled into his arms. Putting his arm round Will, he managed to stagger across the corridor and, with the help of both the cleaners, they got him into the bathroom.

'Thanks,' Phillips leant against the bathroom door, 'you've been a great—'

Before he could finish, the antique dealer appeared at the top of the corridor. 'Are you just going to ignore me? It's outrageous. I will be talking to your superiors.'

Phillips looked at the dealer and back to the cleaners in a total quandary.

'Go on, I'll watch the door. No worries,' the cleaner in charge said kindly, giving a confidence-boosting wink to Phillips. 'He'll be alright.'

Once Phillips had disappeared back into the duty room, the cleaner tried the bathroom door. 'Open up, quick.'

Will opened the door, bemused but in perfect health. The cleaners brushed past him. 'We've no time, get that bucket. It's got a cleaner's uniform in it and a wig.' Seizing the bucket behind the door, Will pulled out the uniform and with some help got dressed in the cleaner's uniform.

The wig was pulled on and a scarf tied over his head. With a scowl from Will, the assistant cleaner gave him a touch of lipstick. After making a few final adjustments, they walked down the corridor to the duty room.

Much to Phillips' relief, the antique dealer's report was just about finished. And the atmosphere was calmer as the dealer made to sign the report.

Just at that moment a little old lady walked into the duty room. 'I've lost my dog,' she wailed. 'She's all I've got. I want a search party.' She dumped on the desk the missing dog's collar and lead. As the collar landed, it knocked over Phillips' mug, spilling tea all over the report.

As Phillips desperately tried to dab the tea-covered report with his handkerchief, another man walked into the duty room. He was holding a youth by the collar. 'I've just caught this vandal trying to break into my car.'

Phillips was unable to speak or move. Outside a firework went off in the car park, the bang making the little old lady scream.

Just then the door from the cells opened and three cleaners, with their buckets, mops and hoover, walked unassumingly through the duty room and out of the front door to the car park. Last to leave, the bossy cleaner turned in the doorway, saying, 'It's all clean and tidy now.' But her comment was lost amongst the shouts of the antique dealer, the wailing old lady, the man wanting action taken about his car and the vandal remonstrating his innocence.

Struggling to regain control, Phillips put his head in his hands. Then something snapped inside him. 'Shut up, all of you!' Immediately there was silence. 'You will each have to wait your turn.' Then, apologetically, he went on, 'Please take a seat and I will be with you as soon as I can.'

With order now restored, Phillips gave the tea-stained report to the antique dealer. It wasn't perfect, but it would do. Without any more fuss, it was signed and the dealer got up to leave. But as he opened the door, two policemen walked in. 'Sorry we're late, traffic was awful from Shrewsbury,' said one of them. 'We had better take your prisoner and be on our way. It'll be just as bad going back.'

Phillips opened and closed his mouth like a goldfish. 'The prisoner… oh no,' he whispered. The policemen, the little old lady and the others watched the panic spread across his face as he rushed for the door. Throwing it open, he disappeared down to the cells.

In his absence, the people who had gathered in the duty room, so keen a few moments ago to make their complaints, slipped into the night. They wouldn't have recognised Sergeant Royson as he walked round the corner. Still worried about the prisoner handover, he had made an excuse to his wife that he had been bleeped, asking him to check into the station.

*

The van that drew up outside Farmers was like any other ordinary family saloon. As the passenger door opened, Roger stepped out of the grocery shop to greet the passenger as he climbed out. The van didn't wait, driving off into the night.

'What's going on? What's this all about?' Will looked round the darkened shop. 'And,' he went on, 'can I take these stupid clothes off now?'

'Yes, yes, there is a lot to explain.' Roger pulled Will into the shop and locked the front door behind them. 'Come with me.'

Will followed Roger down the aisle between the fruit and vegetables to the back of the shop. Behind the screen, sitting between the columns of boxes and cases, were the council members who had reassembled.

Unable to contain herself, the checkout lady from Tesco grabbed Will's hand, kissing it and falling to the ground, and clasped his hands to her cheek.

Roger stepped forward. 'Come on, remember what I said,' gently lifting her back onto her feet.

But the excitement amongst the council was impossible to hide. The talking rolled into laughter as they congratulated each other with hugs and backslapping. Two councillors performed an elfish jig before falling over sacks of potatoes. 'Quiet, everyone, quiet. You will bring the police straight here.' Roger's voice was urgent, but the gathering was gripped by a party mood.

Noticing Roger's worried face, an elderly councillor stood on a crate and, gesturing with outstretched arms, called out in elfish for order. A hush settled as the elder went on in elfish to thank Roger for finding Will and bringing him to them.

'Just a moment,' interrupted Will. 'You're all a bunch of nutters, I am grateful, OK, but I'm not joining a load of junkies talking in a weird language.' Will turned and started off back through the shop to the front door.

Roger caught him up as he struggled with the door handle. 'I'm sorry, it's hard to explain, they have waited a long time for this, please give me a little time to explain.' As Roger was talking, a blue flashing light sped past, making them duck below the window line.

Squatting on the floor, Will wasn't happy. 'Who was the bloke I was banged up with and the girl that said she was my sister? They brought me some clothes. I'll talk to them but not you loonies!'

Will got up from their crouched position on the floor and squared up to Roger, tapping him on the chest. 'If you understand what I am saying, you had better be fast. I'm not hanging about here for long.'

Roger hurried away to behind the screen as Will helped himself to an apple.

Chapter 17

Henry was thinking of his bed, Tom was asleep on the sofa and Flora was already upstairs when there was a knock on the front door.

'Who on earth can that be at this time?' said Milly, going to the door.

'I know it's late,' Lexi was standing on the door mat, 'but I need to see the others. It's pretty urgent.' She twitched her nose, feeling the cold.

'Come in, come in, I think they're watching telly, go and find them. I was off to bed,' said Milly as she turned off some lights.

At the sound of Lexi's voice Tom and Henry appeared, and Flora put her head over the landing balustrade. 'Is that Lexi?' she called.

'I need to talk to you.' For the first time Lexi sounded flustered.

They went back into the study and Flora appeared in her dressing gown.

She told them about the extraordinary success of the night's work. 'Unbelievable. It went like clockwork.

But I think we might not have it so easy now. The town is swarming with police. The other problem is that Will thinks he has been taken by a bunch of madmen. Roger says he will only talk to us.'

'We'd better go, hadn't we?' said Tom, getting up from the sofa.

'You're not going without me,' shouted Flora, disappearing upstairs to get dressed.

Leaving Broad Street, they hurried in the direction of Farmers. They had to shrink into the shadows twice in quick succession as two different police cars flew past them up Broad Street. Deciding that Market Square would be too dangerous, they cut up the alley by the Silver Pear gift shop and then turned left down Raven Lane to Bell Lane.

Halfway down Bell Lane Tom stopped. He lifted his head. 'There is that smell. The goblin smell.' The others stopped to check it too.

'That's all we need,' said Henry.

'It's probably their scouts, trying to ferret out what is going on.' Lexi was matter-of-fact. 'Keep going.'

Before they turned up Mill Street, Lexi went ahead on her own and banged on the door of Farmers. The others waited in the shadows until the door was open and the all-clear was given.

Once in the shop, Roger still had a worried expression and was wringing his hands. 'I've sent all the councillors home, it's too dangerous for them here. Besides, Will thinks they are all mad.'

'Where is he?' asked Flora. 'How is he?'

'The other worry is that there are already reports of goblins in Ludlow.' Roger was only talking to Lexi. 'I don't know how long you... all of you can stay here?'

'I know, we caught their smell on the way here. I need to talk to Will, on my own. I just need a few minutes.' Lexi was now clearly in charge. 'While I do that, the rest of you barricade the front of the shop. Push all the boxes and crates, everything against the door and windows.'

Lexi headed off to the back of the shop whilst the others started to build the defences. It didn't take long for them to move the whole fruit and veg display from around the walls and the centre. They piled it the length of the shop frontage and to ceiling height.

It was during the building of the barricade that somebody tried the front door.

Everybody froze. Outside, voices could be heard. 'Normally you can see into the shop, but they've blocked it up for some reason.' A torch beam filtered through the cracks in the pile of boxes.

Another voice agreed, 'Yeah, that's strange. We'll need a warrant.'

Henry moved slightly so he could see part of the pavement outside the shop. Two policemen were standing together; one was talking on his radio. 'OK, we'll meet you back here in twenty minutes.' The policemen's voices disappeared down Mill Street.

‘Who is going to get us first? Goblins or the police?’ Tom’s attempt at a joke didn’t get a laugh, particularly as Lexi appeared with Will at her side.

‘Will said he will come back to Gwydden with us.’ Lexi kept her voice low. ‘I don’t think he believes a single word I’ve told him, but anything is better than going to prison. What has been going on outside?’

Flora moved a little closer to Will, unable to believe that she was standing close to an elfish king.

Henry whispered, ‘We’ve now got about fifteen minutes before the police return with a war—’

He was cut short by a thundering crash, followed by an explosion of breaking glass. On the cold air that swept into the shop was the distinctive foul reek of goblin.

Lexi turned round, looking at everyone, putting her finger up to her mouth. Nobody moved a muscle.

There was a scrabbling as a goblin tried to open the door. But the crates and boxes were too tightly packed to allow the door to move.

Then there was silence.

Minutes passed as everybody strained to hear any more movement outside the door.

‘This is all some sort of sick joke. I’ll take my chances with the police outside.’ Will wiped his hands on the back of his trousers and started to pull boxes off the barricade.

Roger, with desperation climbing into his voice, said, ‘No, no, you’re right. But you cannot stay here.’

Lexi nodded. ‘But where?’

‘The trap door…’ As Roger turned towards the back of the shop the barricade shuddered as if it had been rammed. Will staggered backwards, his face showing the first signs of fear.

Roger ran to the back of the shop and started to push and pull the pallet that hid the trap door. Henry ran to help him and together they grappled to lift it. Roger knelt down and, feeling just under the lip of the entrance, flicked on a light switch. At the bottom of the steps a naked bulb gave a faint indication of a passage leading away.

‘Hurry, please… you go first, quick.’ Roger beckoned frantically to Will to step down inside the trap door. Everyone had left the front of the shop and was gathered round the open door in the floor. Will, still hesitant, flinched when Flora tried to take his hand. But Flora was insistent and, half pulling and half leading, took Will down the steps.

The barricade juddered again. Boxes tumbled from the top of the defences, scattering tangerines across the floor.

The others followed down the steps until Lexi was the last. She paused.

‘Keep going,’ said Roger, ‘don’t say anything. I will be fine, I know what to do.’

Lexi touched his hand, understanding his sacrifice, and mouthed, ‘Thank you.’

The trap door banged shut over her head. As she hurried after the others she could hear the pallet being pulled back into place.

*

The tunnel walls were lined with stone and there was a hard earthen floor. The lighting wasn't perfect but was good enough for them to avoid the odd puddle.

Lexi called from behind, 'Wait, we must stick together.' Her voice had kept its authority and the others slowed down until she had caught them up.

'Why did they want to break into the shop? What did those things want?' There was an edge of confusion in Will's voice.

'You,' said Lexi. 'Keep going.'

Ahead the dim lighting showed another flight of stone steps, but this time they were leading up. At the top of the stairs was a small arched door, which Flora reached first. She lifted the latch and it swung open easily on well-oiled hinges.

'I don't recognise this,' said Flora. In front of them was a small garden with a neat lawn and well-cared-for beds. Henry was the last out and he, like the others, had to crouch to avoid banging his head. Looking back he could see the tiny door in the stone wall had been cleverly shielded by a protruding buttress and over-hanging ivy.

'I know where we are,' said Tom. 'This is the caretaker's garden.'

'The caretaker of what?' Will's response was short.

'The castle.' Tom pushed open the garden gate and cautiously walked out onto the grassy outer bailey.

‘We can’t stand about here,’ Henry was looking to Lexi, ‘and we cannot go back out through the main gatehouse.’

Tom nodded his agreement. ‘If we go further into the castle we will never get out, we’d be cornered.’ Everyone knew he was right.

‘OK,’ said Lexi, ‘then we make a dash for it out of the castle.’ Keeping close to the garden fence, she led them the short distance to the gatehouse. ‘Stay in the shadows,’ whispered Lexi, ‘pass it round, we’ll go out one at a time.’

They stood for a moment, straining all their senses to smell, see or hear goblins. Across the Market Square came the odd flurry of snow. The skeletal frames of the market stalls added a loneliness to the deserted square.

‘Henry, I think you should go first? When you get outside the gates, turn left and follow the path down to the trees. We’ll all meet there.’ Lexi patted him on the back. ‘Then I will send Flora and Will together, and the rest of us will come on, one by one, OK?’

Henry disappeared, his figure soon lost as the snow flurries turned to bigger flakes. The others waited. But there was only silence. ‘OK, you two, you know where you are going. Henry will be waiting for you.’ Lexi was about to dispatch Flora and Will when she gripped Flora’s shoulder, pulling her back into the shadows.

The snow had blown itself out, leaving the square covered in a white veneer. Against the white background they could all see what had stopped Lexi from sending the next two.

Darting in between the empty stalls were the unmistakable silhouettes of three or four goblins probing forward in the direction of the castle. Even their hideous smell reached them on the icy air.

'We can't go out there,' Flora's voice was full of panic, 'and we've lost Henry. They'll get him, won't they?'

'We've got to get Henry back. Lexi, go and find him.' Tom, too, sounded frightened. 'We will make a diversion, on the castle walls. We'll get up over there, on the far right, and make sure they see us.'

Tom's plan was accepted silently. Lexi waited until Tom and the others had reached a flight of stone steps that led up to the ramparts. Once on the walls, Lexi saw them banging and rubbing their hands together in an obvious way to keep warm. The noise carried, catching the goblins' attention. They reacted immediately, moving over towards Castle Lodge to investigate and taking their attention off the castle entrance.

Lexi slipped out from the protection of the gatehouse shadows and headed down the path that Henry had taken minutes earlier. As she neared the trees she called out softly. In answer, Henry stepped out from the shadows of a yew tree.

'Where are Flora and W—'

Lexi put her finger to her mouth, stopping Henry in mid-sentence. 'Shhh… I will tell you in a sec, but we are going back… no questions, let's go.'

Together they ran back up the path, arriving, out of breath, by the tourist kiosk outside the gatehouse. As they scanned the square before making their next move, a cry went up from the direction of Castle Lodge.

'Oh no,' said Henry as he counted at least a dozen goblins milling about on the pavement. The leader of the goblin group was pointing at Lexi and Henry, and with wild shouts they started to head in their direction.

Lexi touched Henry's arm and without a word they sprinted for the gatehouse.

Henry could hear the slap of goblin feet on the road behind him, but he didn't dare look back. They were both through the gateway when Lexi stopped and turned. 'Quick, close the gates.' Henry had never thought about the old gates.

Together they had one of the ancient studded doors half closed when Tom, Will and Flora miraculously appeared. They started to close the other heavy door. The gap was narrowing fast when the goblin pack, screaming and howling, slammed into it.

The first two goblins almost got through the doors. In anticipation, Will stood back to greet them. With a hard kick and several devastating punches, he sent the goblins sprawling backwards. But the goblins still fought on, pushing, beating and scratching through the gap, at one time grabbing Flora's arm as they struggled face to face. Flora was more angry than frightened. Alert to the danger, Will reached through the gap, grabbing the goblin by its throat and shaking the creature until it released Flora for fear of its own life.

Whilst they were outnumbered two to one, it was their combined weight that made the difference. Inch by inch they closed the doors despite more goblins arriving to join the fray. At last they managed to swing a heavy iron bar into place, locking the doors.

As they leant against the massive doors, they could feel the crash of cudgels behind their backs and reverberating cries of angry goblins baying for their blood.

*

The snow was again flying horizontally as they headed across the grass to the drawbridge over the moat. Going further into the castle was madness, but there were no other options. They hurried through the keep into the inner bailey. They paused to listen for the sound of their pursuers. At least they were now sheltered from the snow, but overhead the sharp wind moaned between ruined towers and walls, making it harder to pick out any sound of danger.

'Let's try and get out of the wind.' Flora knew the castle better than the others. 'I cannot think properly out here.'

The others didn't say anything. They followed her past the little circular chapel, reaching the shelter of a large rectangular room that was open to the sky.

Once, the room might have been a great hall hung with tapestries and warmed with roaring fireplaces. Now they settled into a corner, huddled like sheep for warmth and protection.

'They won't take long to find us, will they?' Flora's voice was matter-of-fact.

No one answered.

'What will they do to us?' Flora was talking to herself, while the others were lost in their own thoughts.

Only Will spoke of what was going through his head. 'Funny thing, really, escape from a police cell one moment, to be torn apart by goblins the next. I wish my mates were here…' His voice trailed off.

Henry reached down inside his shirt to find his flute and, after rubbing it affectionately between his fingers, he started to play the little instrument.

Will smiled. 'That's nice.'

As Henry played, the noise of the wind outside died and a warmth crept into the open room. From somewhere a light, a burning torch, flickered across the bare walls.

Lexi stood up.

'What is going on?' Flora asked curiously, as she got up as well.

'I think…' said Lexi, and then fell quiet.

Flora looked up. Above her there was no longer open sky. Instead there was a wooden ceiling. As they turned to look down the room, there was now a door where before there was a gaping hole.

Henry stopped playing. 'What's happening?'

'I know,' whispered Flora, then, with more confidence, 'I know.'

'What?' shouted the others.

'The castle, the castle is coming alive, it's coming back to save us,' said Flora, dancing across the floor.

Chapter 18

Just as Flora finished speaking, the large door at the end of the room swung open with a crash. The noise brought everybody to their feet. Flora took a step forward, then started walking to the door.

'Who is there?' she asked.

In the doorway stood a knight. He was medium height, bareheaded, with a full beard and long straggly hair. He was dressed simply in a tunic over chain mail. Wrapped twice round his waist was a leather belt. From it hung a sword with an ugly hilt: a working sword in a plain scabbard. One hand rested on the hilt; the other arm was hidden by a shield half his own size. Behind him there were more soldiers, the light spreading from their torches across the ceiling of the room.

Without speaking, the knight turned and beckoned that they were to follow him.

Through the door he led the way across a hallway and, without stopping, headed up a spiral staircase.

The soldiers with torches brought up the rear. As they climbed, Henry, who was last, couldn't help noticing how the castle had changed. He ran his hand over well-pointed walls. Under his feet were smooth, dry, stone treads. And there were torches burning in brackets about every tenth step. Pausing to peer out of an arrow slit, the scene below in the inner bailey took his breath away. When they had crossed the same ground earlier, looking for shelter, it had been a desolate place bound by grim, ruined walls. Now it was thronged with armed soldiers gathering their battle equipment, saddling horses and damping down campfires. The smell of woodsmoke drifted up to him and borne on the cold air came the snap of orders and the soldiers' curses as they struggled in response to make ready. Above the melee the ruined skyline had been replaced with solid walls, turrets, tiled roofs and ramparts.

Having fallen behind, Henry hurried to catch up with the others. He found them, transfixed, at the top of the spiral stairs.

Before them was the great hall. For its size and height, and vaulted ceiling, the room was inviting. A huge open fire threw out welcome heat. The boarded floor was strewn with animal skins and furs. And on the walls were rich rugs and finely woven tapestries. The room was well lit. There were candles on pedestal stands, more wall-mounted torches and the fire added a warm, orangey mood.

In the centre of the great hall was a long table laden with food and drink. There were haunches of venison, legs of ham, meat pies, loaves of bread and earthenware jugs. Plates were piled with food, knives and forks poised for use. But the chairs had been pushed back as if the occupants had left in a hurry.

'Where is everyone?' Flora voiced everyone else's thoughts.

Whilst they took in the great chamber, the silent knight had walked down the room and opened a door in the corner, to the far right of the fireplace. From the open door came the sounds of a commotion. Then laughter followed by happy noises.

'I'm so sorry to keep you all waiting.' Pushing past the knight and sweeping into the chamber came a young woman. 'But since your call, you can imagine it has been bedlam here.'

Her fresh young face was lit by a broad smile. A mane of fair hair tumbled down her back, contrasting with the deep damson colour of her dress. And showing on her forehead was a thin gold crown.

'I am Elen, daughter of Prince Cadell.' Standing in front of them, she gave a small curtsey. 'My father is on his way.'

Will interrupted, 'I am completely lost in all of this. We need to—'

'Hang on, Will.' Lexi stepped in.

'Hang on! Will's right, what is going on here?' Tom sounded uneasy.

‘OK, OK, but let Elen finish. Elen, this has caught us all by surprise. But as a child I remember the name Prince Cadell. Is this anything to do with the legend of Idwal?’

‘Yes, it is. You’re right. Perhaps I should quickly explain?’ Elen walked over to the fire to warm her hands.

Lexi nodded.

‘The legend of Idwal,’ began Elen. ‘Many, many years ago there was a battle, the battle of all battles, between elves and goblins. It was after the death of King Artan, which was a bad time for elfish people. The elves were surrounded here, in what is now Ludlow, and there was no escape from certain massacre. At the head of the elfish army was a prince called Idwal. With no choices left to him, he decided to ask for help from the castle, the human world. For elves this is unheard of, against everything elves are taught.’

Henry pulled up a chair and sat down by the table. Lexi, Tom and Flora did the same. But Will moved closer to the fire, to stand by Elen.

‘Ludlow Castle was in the hands of a man called Red Robert. “Red” because he had a fiery temper. And he turned out to be as evil as the goblins. Instead of helping, he imprisoned Idwal and the elves in the foulest of dungeons imaginable. There they would have rotted away had it not been for Red Robert’s daughter. She visited the elves every day, slipping them whatever food she could find them. With her was a boy. It was obvious he was not her child, for he was fair whilst she was dark. She had once told Idwal that the boy had royal blood. And on his leg was a strange mark, which she couldn't explain.

'In time, Idwal fell in love with Red Robert's daughter, but her evil father soon found out. He had them brought to him and told them that he would set the elves free in exchange for Idwal's life. Idwal knew he had no choice and agreed to Red Robert's demand.

'But the night before Idwal was to be sent to the scaffold, Red Robert's daughter drugged him and disguised herself in his clothes. Robert, without knowing it, executed his own daughter. Idwal escaped that same morning with the elves when they were set free. But as he left the little boy ran after him, asking to be taken with him. Idwal ignored him, frightened that he would be discovered.

'After Idwal's safe return home, he came to realise that the boy was the lost son of King Artan. Idwal died shortly afterwards, a broken man. On his deathbed he swore an elfin oath that there would always be an elfish army waiting in the castle should the lost king ever return.'

Elen's voice cracked as she finished the story. She looked shyly at Will, giving him a knowing smile.

'So,' said Will, 'are you saying—'

Cutting Will off in mid-sentence was the sound of heavy steps from behind the door in the corner. In the doorway appeared an older man dressed in a long cloak. His ancient face was pink with cold and his long grey hair and beard were still covered in melting snow. Undoing the clasp at his neck, he shook off the great cloak as he walked to the fire, throwing it on the back of a chair. Under the cloak he was clothed in a dark velvet tunic. From an ornate belt, woven from golden strands hung a sword. The hilt of the sword was finely crafted and set with precious stones. But it was not the only sign of his high office. He too wore a simple gold crown.

Elen curtseyed. 'Father—'

'Where is he? Which is the one? We have waited long enough for this day.' Prince Cadell looked kindly at the apprehensive group in front of him. 'Come on, we haven't any time.'

'It's Will, it's him.' Flora dug Will in the ribs. 'Say something, Will.'

Prince Cadell turned his attention to Will. 'Well?'

'Lexi says he has got a funny mark on his left leg.' Flora circled Will and then made a grab for his leg.

Will sidestepped her lunge, looking crossly at Prince Cadell. 'If I show you, can we then go?' said Will. 'I want out of this place; I can take my chances outside.'

Prince Cadell put his hand on Will's shoulder. 'Show me,' demanded the prince.

Will rolled up his trouser leg, baring the mark on his leg. Immediately, Prince Cadell knelt on one knee and bowed his head. Princess Elen joined her father by his side.

'It is true!' The prince's voice was husky with emotion.

Will looked startled, glancing over at the others for support.

'I told you,' Flora laughed, 'Will is the lost—'

From the direction of the outer bailey came the wild cries of men and the clatter of hooves on cobbles. At the same moment the same silent knight reappeared, beckoning urgently to Prince Cadell.

'Come with me,' called Prince Cadell with a fleeting look over his shoulder at Will. 'Unfortunately,' he continued with a note of sarcasm, 'it seems that the goblins have heard the news and they too want to celebrate your return.'

*

They left the great hall by the same staircase. In the hallway servants handed them each a thick woollen cloak. Through the open door they could see it was snowing hard.

The inner bailey was still a mass of elfish soldiers. But they were now organised, dressed and ready for battle. A tingling mix of fear and excitement vibrated in the air. There were spearmen, men with longbows, men with sword and shield. Warhorses champed at their bits, their riders soothing their mounts with steadying words. On the ramparts above their heads, armed elves stood guard, glowing braziers catching their silhouettes as they patrolled in and out of the black of night.

Outside in the biting wind they were thankful for their warm cloaks. As they stood waiting, four elves stepped forward to join the party. Their physique and fine uniforms singled them out as different from other soldiers.

'We have just got our own bodyguards,' murmured Henry.

Sharp orders parted the way for Prince Cadell and his entourage as they made their way out through the entrance tower. Here was another sight to greet them. The outer bailey was more like a shanty town. The green grass had disappeared. In its place was a brown quagmire crammed with orderless shacks and hovels. Panic had set in as elfish women and children were streaming towards the keep. In the rush, possessions were dropped, cooking fires were overturned and half-cooked food was tipped into the mud. Babies wailed, and dogs snapped as they fought over trodden scraps.

'Do you want to go on?' asked Prince Cadell.

'Of course!' retorted Will, but the others looked more doubtful.

Fighting against the tide of people, the party headed right towards the outer bailey walls. The strong arms of soldiers pulled them out of the crowd and up stone steps. On top of the battlement, Prince Cadell paused to check they were all present and correct, then led the way in the direction of the front gate. Below them the elfish garrison was now taking up new positions in the outer bailey, the silent discipline of the soldiers contrasting with the earlier chaos. Reaching the main gates, the group climbed to a parapet between two turrets. From here they could see anything that moved in the Market Square.

The driving bitter snow had turned to big, floating flakes. The square was in darkness; there were no lights from any houses. The snow reflected a chilly quietness and the soldiers on the wall shifted nervously, peering into nothingness.

Tom saw them first.

From the shadows of the town, they spread like spilt ink across the snow. From every street came seething hordes of goblins. Some beat long cylindrical drums, others held burning torches and, in the fiery light, forests of ugly pikes stood out above their heads. In their hands were curved swords; battle axes and crossbows were slung over shoulders. The monotonous beat of the drums, the slap of goblin feet and their stench soon reached their ears and noses to send shivers down their spines.

'Look at the goblins in the front,' said Flora. 'What are we going to do?'

The leading goblins carried scaling ladders and grappling hooks. As Flora spoke they rushed forward towards the castle gates. In support, goblins armed with crossbows fired a volley of lethal bolts that flew in a shallow arc straight towards them. Prince Cadell barked for everyone to crouch tightly behind the rampart wall. The guards on the wall lifted their shields. The shower of bolts rattled against the stonework, but some found their first targets; the cries of wounded and dying sliced through air.

Nervously lifting their heads above the battlements, the scene below filled the onlookers with new terror. The scaling parties had reached the castle walls and ladders were being thrust forward into place. Grappling hooks clattered too against stone walls and were pushed firmly into place as the assailants started to climb up. Some goblins hurled their torches over the walls. Most fell short, but several cleared the walls to land in amongst the shacks. Fires quickly took hold.

But it was the sight at the far side of the square that brought more gasps of dismay. In the second wave were siege machines. Accompanying carts carried rocks and others were specially adapted to carry cauldrons that held a steaming liquid. In the middle between the siege machines, Henry pointed out a different contraption. Nobody needed to be told it was a battering ram.

In front of the siege machines rode a goblin on a black horse, dressed all in black armour. Milling around the legs of the horse was a pack of creamy-coloured wolves. Now and again the black-dressed goblin cracked a long whip, lashing out at his goblin soldiers. And the wolves howled, biting any goblin that fell under the cut of the whip.

Even from where they stood, they could see the black-dressed goblin's bright yellow eyes.

'You are not staying here, it is much worse than I first imagined.' Prince Cadell took Will by the arm. 'Come on, quick, all of you.'

With Prince Cadell in the lead they hurried back, weaving in and out of the elfish soldiers on the wall. As he went, the prince gave words of encouragement, calling soldiers by their names to stand fast.

'Who was that?' shouted Will. 'Who was that evil-looking thing on the horse?'

Without stopping or turning round, Prince Cadell said nothing and carried on until they had arrived back at the drawbridge leading to the inner bailey. Then they paused to look back. Goblins were already gaining the ramparts of the outer bailey and their numbers were growing by the minute. Elves were locked in furious hand-to-hand fighting as they attempted to stem the tide. As they watched, a boulder from a siege machine flew in a high lazy arc, smashing into shacks and hovels, which were now well alight. Another followed, then another, fizzing through the air.

'Who was he?' Will asked again when they had caught their breath.

'That was,' said Prince Cadell, 'none other than Sla. He must have come to personally supervise your capture.'

'Where is Henry?' Tom asked.

‘He was with us when we left the main gates,’ Flora answered anxiously.

Without a word to anyone Lexi started back towards the ramparts. ‘You cannot go back,’ shouted Prince Cadell against the increasing noise of the battle. ‘It’s far too dangerous.’

‘I’m not leaving him,’ cried Lexi.

‘You haven’t anything to protect yourself with. Here, have this sword and my bow… please.’ Prince Cadell pulled the bow from his back. ‘And the quiver. There is a white arrow in there too. Fire it back to us if you find him and need help.’

She took the bow and quiver and was gone, lost in the smoke drifting from the burning shacks.

‘Nobody else go. We stay together.’ The prince shepherded them through into the safety on the inner bailey. ‘I will send my bodyguards after her. But everyone else, don’t think about going back.’

*

Lexi made good progress, but the closer she got to the main gates the harder it became. Acrid smoke stung her eyes. Elves tugged at her clothes trying to prevent her from getting closer to the fighting. And it was blowing hard driven snow.

Undeterred she pressed on, climbing up onto the ramparts.

From nowhere sprung a goblin. The creature swung

a double-handed axe above its head and, with yellow eyes gleaming, it brought the crescent-shaped blade sweeping down towards her. But Lexi was faster than the goblin. She neatly sidestepped the blow and the blade sent sparks flying as it crashed against the stone wall. She took quick advantage as the goblin tried to recover its balance. With all her strength she grabbed its shoulder straps and swung the creature round till it lost its footing and fell backwards over the edge of the battlements.

Not wishing to be caught unawares again, Lexi looked about for a sword. Moving slowly forward she stepped over the bodies of elves and goblins that were lying twisted on the walkway. Without fuss, she prised a sword from the lifeless hand of an elf and a handy dagger from a dead goblin.

Below her, in the outer bailey, there was mayhem. The goblins must have broken through the gates with the battering ram. A pitched battle was now raging with the main elfish garrison. The fires from the burning shacks lit the faces of elves and goblins alike. Lexi could see every grim detail of the onslaught being dealt by the goblins.

Then she saw Henry.

He was being dragged backwards by two goblins, towards the main gates and out of the castle. He wasn't struggling and Lexi could see blood on his left arm. In only a few minutes he would be through the gates and gone.

Lexi stumbled the last stretch of the walkway and found the steps leading up to the vantage point between the two turrets. She surprised several goblins but dodged past them in the confusion. Climbing the steps two at a time, she reached the parapet. Here there were still grappling irons left in place. Selecting the nearest, Lexi gathered up the rope and unhooked the iron anchor. Looking over the wall, she secured the anchor and threw out the rope. The goblins, confused a moment ago, caught up with her. The first lunged with a pike that Lexi turned away with her sword. The goblin held on to the pike but, to her attacker's surprise, Lexi grabbed the shaft, pulling it towards her. The goblin came too, running itself onto Lexi's dagger. The other goblin started a second attack. But it was half hearted. Lexi swung the pike round her head, letting go so it flew at her assailant. It missed. But the goblin, realising his match, disappeared in search of reinforcements.

Taking her chance, Lexi swung her legs over the wall. Holding on with her hands and wrapping her legs round the rope, she slithered down the rope to the ground.

She fell the last few feet, landing in a jarring heap. As she jumped to her feet, the goblins and Henry were just a few feet from her. But instead of putting up a fight, Henry's capturers stood frozen to the spot.

A wolf brushed past Lexi and circled Henry's prone body. The goblins slunk away, whimpering, as the rest of the pack of wolves appeared.

Henry stirred, shaking his head, as he sat up.

'You OK?' asked Lexi. Despite the wolves, Lexi knelt down by Henry.

'Just about,' Henry whispered. 'Somebody must have hit me over the head and it hurts like hell. Where are we?'

'We are in the middle of a battle; the goblins have...' Lexi paused, cocking her head. 'You had better take this dagger.'

The noise of battle had disappeared and the fighting had stopped. The shacks had been reduced to embers, spindles of smoke curled skywards and snow had already settled on the bodies strewn across the mud. In the background the remaining goblin army stood motionless, watching and waiting.

The wolves continued to prowl round them both. The largest wolf, the leader of the pack, started to howl. It was followed by another and then another until all of them were howling in unison.

The crack of a whip brought instant silence.

'So I was right. Humans.' The voice had come from nowhere. The words were spoken in an evil, grainy voice. 'Humans' was said with deep loathing.

Above them towered Sla. The red nostrils of his black horse flared as it pawed the ground.

'Where is he?' Sla slowly levelled his whip at Lexi. 'He belongs to me.'

Sla's yellow eyes smouldered with evil, sending cold rivers of fear into Lexi and Henry. Under his war helmet his face was grotesque, his goblin nose covered in warts, his rotten teeth nearly the same colour as his eyes. His black armour, covered in an oily sheen, moved and glistened like a snake. In a gloved hand he held a long, curved sword. From it dripped blood, forming a pool on the ground that the wolves eagerly drank.

'I will get him.' Lexi's voice sounded as if it was in a trance.

'Lexi, what are you doing? How could you…?' said Henry in disbelief.

'Shut up, Henry.' Lexi cut him short, adding, in an icy voice, 'We must do as we are told.'

Henry slumped to the ground, unable to comprehend Lexi's apparent treachery. But she showed no feelings. She pulled Henry up by the collar, forcing him to stand, and started walking back through the main gate into the outer bailey. Sla followed, on his horse, several paces behind.

Now fifty paces from the drawbridge, Lexi stopped. She moved the bow from her back and reached into the quiver.

'I will fire a white arrow over the wall,' Lexi said, turning to Sla, still sounding as if she had been drugged. 'It will be an order to them to surrender.'

Sla let out a murderous laugh and his goblin soldiers banged their weapons on their shields, gloating at the elfish capitulation. 'Just get on with it,' he hissed.

Lexi let the arrow fly. Henry buried his head in the ground, unable to watch what he thought was their betrayal.

*

In the inner bailey elfish morale had evaporated. The heavy casualties at the hands of the goblins in the outer bailey and the withdrawal across the drawbridge into the inner bailey had been a disaster.

Tom, Flora and Will watched forlornly as Prince Cadell tried to rally and reorganise his soldiers. On top of the casualties, the news of Henry's capture and Lexi's disappearance had spread through all ranks. The urge to fight had gone.

Then the white arrow landed.

Will ran to it, snatching it from the ground. 'What does this mean? Has she found him?'

Prince Cadell took the arrow from Will, turning it over in his hand. A nervous chatter started from the weary elves. 'Yes, it is mine.' His voice was unable to hide his excitement. 'She must need our help.'

The prince moved to rally his troops, but there was still little appetite for another fight even after the news spread of the white arrow. He came back more downcast than before. 'We are beaten.' His voiced faded, resigned that their fate was sealed.

'No, we are not beaten,' shouted Will as he ran to the nearest soldiers standing dejectedly with their horses.

Picking a horse, he quickly mounted it and, bending down, beckoned to a soldier to give him a sword.

'Are you not part of the legend of Idwal? You are, I know you are. You were brought up on the legend. Remember how your mother used to tell you your king would come back? That day is here; that day has come.' Will stopped and, with the sword, ripped his trouser leg open to reveal his birthmark. The nearest soldiers gasped, and as Will rode down the line of elves, the gasps turned to shouts and the shouting became a roar.

Within a few minutes the despondency had vanished and, at the head of his horsemen, Will demanded the gates be opened. The huge doors were swung inwards and with a rattle the drawbridge was dropped. At a gallop Will led the elfish charge across the moat and back into battle.

Sla watched as the gates opened, expecting a meek surrender party to emerge and beg for his mercy. Instead he was faced with a cavalry charge that moved at such speed it left him standing, unable to move in any direction. The elfish charge went past him and on to the goblin army that too was immobilised by the surprise attack.

Seeing Sla, Will pulled his horse up. Standing in his stirrups, he caught sight of Lexi and Henry. They were crouching down by Sla, kept at heel by his pack of wolves.

Without hesitation, Will spurred his horse forward, heading straight for Sla. Other horsemen saw Will's action and, with elfish battle cries, joined in the attack. Sla let out a terrible curse then turned away, realising that the initiative was lost. The pack of wolves scattered and bounded after their master.

'Get on, quick.' Will stopped short next to Lexi and leant down to give her his arm.

Lexi shook her head. 'Henry first, he's hurt.'

Together they pushed and pulled Henry up into position behind Will. Lexi slapped the horse's flank and they were off back over the drawbridge. Another elfish horseman pulled Lexi effortlessly up to sit behind him and they followed Will back into the inner bailey.

*

Celebrations in the great chamber had already begun when they arrived back in the room. Elen took Henry away to dress his wounded arm, but the others were made the centre of the party. Outside the soldiers were returning from securing the castle and rounding up the last of the goblin prisoners. They too were in the mood for partying. Dancing had started and casks of wine had been brought up from the cellars.

'This will be a feast to beat all feasts.' Prince Cadell glowed.

'Prince Cadell, I'm sorry, really sorry, but we must go.' Lexi knew she would be unpopular. 'It is still not safe here, Sla may be back. He won't give up that easily. And we have to get Will back to Gwydden.'

Prince Cadell looked crestfallen for a moment then smiled as he accepted Lexi's decision. 'Yes, yes, you're right, of course. That is more important than a party. But leave quietly so as not to disappoint the others.'

Lexi gathered up the others discreetly when Henry had reappeared. But for his bandaged arm, he looked none the worse for his ordeal. With the party in full swing, Prince Cadell opened a side door behind a curtain and led the group down a narrow spiral staircase. At the bottom he pulled out a large iron ring, on which there was one heavy key.

'I haven't used this key for… hundreds of years,' he muttered to himself. The door opened stiffly on rusty hinges and cold air swept in past them.

'Goodbye, thank you, take care, all of you, and good luck in your journey.' Prince Cadell shook each of them by the hand. But when it came to Will's turn, he fell to his knees, pressing Will's hands to his old face. 'Come back, please,' he whispered, unable to hold back his tears.

Chapter 19

It was eerily quiet outside the castle. For a moment they all stood motionless, each of them going through a sense of loss. Over their heads it was a brilliant starry night and underfoot the snow already had a crisp, frosty covering.

Henry took several paces down the slope to look back at the castle. Above him loomed the garderobe tower. He was half expecting lights and laughter from the party to spill out of the windows. But they were blank and lifeless, like empty eye sockets.

Nobody said anything, although they all felt it. The castle was a ruin again.

Eventually Tom said, 'Come on, let's get down to the road, I think it's over there.'

They slid and stumbled down the bank, pushing their way through scrub and brambles before they found a footpath that led steeply down to the road.

'This is Dinham,' said Flora. 'Which way?'

Before anybody had an answer there was the sound of a siren from the direction of the town and a moment later a police car with its blue light flashing hurried down the hill and crossed over the river by Dinham Bridge.

'I had forgotten about them,' said Will wearily. 'What do we do next?'

'We are going to get you to Gwydden. That's the plan,' answered Lexi, 'but the town is obviously dangerous.'

'What's the alternative?' questioned Tom. 'We need some transport.'

'If we had a mobile we could call for a taxi but they wouldn't take us right into the middle of Mortimer Forest,' suggested Henry.

'I've still got my mobile,' said Flora, waving it in her hand.

'You are amazing, Flora,' said Henry, 'and I've just had an idea. Call a taxi and ask him to meet us outside Underhill's, just along here on the right.'

'What's the big idea then?' asked Lexi. 'We'd better know.'

'The taxi's on its way,' butted in Flora. 'I hope somebody has got some money?'

'I've got a tenner,' said Henry. 'It won't be more than that. If we go to the stables at Downton, we can borrow the stable pick-up truck; I know where the key is. It won't be missed for an hour or so and the police won't think of looking for us up there.'

Nobody had any objections and after a short wait the taxi arrived.

'You lot been to a fancy-dress party then?' quipped the taxi driver in a jolly voice. The remark startled them, for they were forgetting they were still dressed in their cloaks; Lexi even had her bow and quiver over her shoulder.

'Umm, yes,' joked Lexi, 'we've been to quite a party tonight.'

The others laughed nervously too.

'You know I'm not meant to carry five people, don't you?' said the taxi driver half seriously. 'The town is crawling with police tonight. There is an escaped prisoner on the loose, so I've heard. And I don't want my licence taken away from me.'

'We're not going into the town. We just want to get to Downton – will this cover it?' Henry held out his ten-pound note.

'Yeah, OK, but make sure one of you keeps your head down if we see a police car.'

Tom jumped into the front and the rest squeezed into the back.

It wasn't much more than a few miles to Downton, but the taxi driver wasn't in a hurry. Partly to avoid attention by keeping his speed down and partly because he was talking so much. He kept up a running commentary on his own experiences at parties. 'Mind you,' he started as they turned off the main road, 'I've never been to a party dressed as a knight like you lot

– original, that is. Where do you get the kit from? I might give them a ring.'

Flora opened her mouth to answer, but Will slipped his hand over her mouth.

The lanes were cloaked in snow. Aiming between the hedges, they cautiously followed in the tracks of a previous vehicle that had braved the conditions. But negotiating the drive up to the stables proved to be a more hazardous affair. The taxi slithered and twitched its way forward with the driver coaxing the car with, 'Not that way, please,' or, 'Come back this way, my girl.'

Eventually, they drew up in the stable yard, which was covered in a good three inches of snow. Making sure not to slam the taxi doors, they thanked the driver and headed for the red pick-up that was parked by the office.

As the noise of the taxi died in the distance, Lexi held her hand up as a signal for everyone to stand still. They all listened, waiting for somebody to turn up and ask them what was going on so late. From somewhere came the faint sound of music. Only the horses seemed interested. They watched in silence over the stable doors, their nostrils puffing warm breath into the cold night air. Otherwise the night remained undisturbed.

'The key is normally on top of the front left wheel,' whispered Tom as he walked round the pick-up, brushing the snow from the windscreen. Grinning, he held up a well-worn wooden tag from which hung two keys. Stepping round to the driver's side, Tom opened the door and slid in behind the steering wheel.

'Climb in,' called Tom, turning the key.

The engine didn't respond. There wasn't even a reassuring clunk of it turning over.

'It's probably the battery. Can you check it, Henry?' Tom pulled the lever to open the bonnet. Henry quickly swung out of the back and lifted the bonnet up. Almost immediately he let it down again, closing it gently.

Henry bent down by Tom's window and said quietly, 'There is no battery.'

'I don't believe it.' Tom opened the bonnet again and jumped out of the car.

'What is the matter?' Lexi's whisper sounded edgy.

'There isn't a battery,' said Henry with a shrug.

'He's right, would you believe it.' Tom closed the bonnet and sat on the front of the car, looking away from the others.

'Any brainwaves?' Will joined in as if he was speaking for everybody.

'I've no idea,' replied Henry.

After a silence, Tom spoke up. 'There is one other way.'

Everyone turned, looking at him with relief. Tom went on, 'You know, Henry, it is, or rather they are staring us in the face?'

Henry looked at Tom for a moment and then the penny dropped. 'No, Tom, that's out of the question.

We would never get away with it, you're mad.'

But Tom was adamant. 'What's the alternative? If we stay here any longer, somebody will find us, the police, goblins, I don't know. We'll lose Will. Why throw it all away at this stage?'

'What are you two talking about?' asked Flora crossly.

'Tom's idea,' said Henry slowly, 'is to take the horses!'

There was a hush as the idea sank in.

'That's brilliant, we could do it,' said Flora, getting out of the back of the pick-up. 'They're racehorses, aren't they? We'll get there in no time.'

'What do you think, Lexi?' Henry looked at her for help.

'Tom's right. If we stay here any longer we will be caught. We must put Will first. I think the horses are our only chance.' By her voice, Henry knew that she had made her mind up.

'Heaven help us if we are caught,' sighed Henry.

'Henry, get the saddles and bridles,' responded Tom. 'The other key on the pick-up key ring is for the tack-room door.' Tom went off to check which horses he thought were best suited for the job and then joined Henry in the tack room. They worked quickly to collect the tack and, working together, they went from box to box, saddling up five horses.

The others waited in the shadows by the office until Tom and Henry called them over to take a horse each.

'Will, this grey is yours. She is called Misty. Take her out of the yard and we'll mount up a bit further down the road.'

Henry handed over two more horses, giving Flora Parlour Game and Lexi Lord Moose. Taking the horses by their bridles, they both followed Will out of the yard. Tom brought up the rear with his horse, Rakalackey, and Henry's, Jakari. Nothing stirred, the snow muffling the horses' hooves.

Well away from the stable yard they found a place to mount up.

'Who's going to help me? This horse is enormous, I need a leg-up or even a crane.' Flora giggled. Will got Henry to hold Misty and catapulted Flora though the air into the tiny racing saddle.

The others took turns to give each other a leg-up. Tom was the last and climbed a fallen tree trunk to help himself up into the saddle.

'Everyone lengthen your stirrups, they are too short,' commanded Tom in a low voice.

Once everyone was comfortable they set off with Tom in front. The others followed in line with Henry in the rear. To start with the horses had been lethargic, almost as if they resented being taken from their warm stables. Now they snorted and pulled at the reins, sensing the importance of the task that lay ahead of them.

From the stables they headed due north across open fields. They needed to skirt some farm cottages that Tom knew had several restless dogs, itching for an excuse to bark. Leaving the cottages behind, they swung west to cross the lane that ran along the top of Whitbatch. The wind was biting and they pulled their long cloaks about them, grateful again for their warmth.

Before they crossed the road, Tom went ahead. He dismounted to open a gate and to listen. He needn't have worried. The wind had swept the road and sculptured graceful, curved drifts that in places spilled over the tops of the hedges. No car, however good, could have used the road that night.

Tom had judged the point they had to cross the road perfectly. Opposite was the footpath, the fingerpost sticking up clearly with a cap of snow. The path headed north-west towards a straggle of houses at Hayton's Bent. Tom's plan was to follow the path until they reached the first house, then they would turn left on the path to Woodlands Farm and on down the hill to Stanton Lacy. He was feeling more relaxed. They were now away from Downton and the horses were behaving perfectly well.

Holding his horse by the bridle, Tom moved into the middle of the road and motioned to the others to follow. But he stopped by the fingerpost. On the ground there were paw prints and when he looked up the path there were more. More than a couple of dogs could make. And they were fresh. Then they all heard it. From down the footpath they were planning to take, a wolf howled.

Rakalackey reared up, her terrified whinny stabbing the cold air. The other horses tried to scatter, Henry and Lexi's horses turning back the way they had come towards the safety of their stables. Flora lost control of Parlour Game, who ran through the gate and into drifts until they were wallowing in deep snow. She was too frightened to say anything, let alone scream for help.

Rakalackey's violent response wrenched the reins out of Tom's hands. Will was already moving across the road as Rakalackey reacted to the wolf's howl. As her reins flew through the air, Will was close enough to catch them.

'Steady, steady.' Will's soothing words and strong grip brought the quivering horse under control.

Henry was quick to rein in Jakari and also managed to catch Lord Moose by his bridle. Both horses were jittery, but Henry steered them both back to the gate, which he closed after them.

'Thanks, Henry.' Lexi's voice was breathless. 'That was Sla's wolves again, wasn't it?'

'Mmm, yes… I really thought—' Henry's answer was cut short.

'Hey, what about me?' shouted Flora, finding her voice. 'Get me out of here.' Parlour Game was still floundering and Flora was looking increasingly agitated.

'I've got Rakalackey, go and help her,' Will barked at Tom.

Tom gingerly approached the terrified pair as they struggled to free themselves. Tom had ridden out on Parlour Game many times so, as he talked to her in gentle tones, she recognised his voice. Very slowly he reached out for her reins that were dangling loose.

With the reins safely gathered up, he gave Parlour Game a reassuring pat and started to coax her round to get her out of the deep snow. She lurched and, with added encouragement from Flora and Tom's firm hand, they staggered back onto the road.

'Henry, bring Rakalackey over to the gate so I can get back on, would you?' Tom jumped onto the gate and, while Henry held Rakalackey steady, he sprang back into the saddle.

'OK, everyone, let's—' Tom's words of encouragement broke off as the wolf howled again. This time much closer.

Flora and Parlour Game bolted down the lane in the direction of Ludlow. The others could hear Flora cursing and remonstrating, but there was no stopping her horse. She just had to hang on.

'We'll have to follow her,' shouted Henry. The other horses didn't need to be spurred into action and they were quickly flying down the snowy lane in pursuit of Flora.

Flora's brave attempts to slow down Parlour Game had some effect and it wasn't long before they caught up with her. Tom manoeuvred himself in front again and slowed his horse into a trot. The others followed suit and order was restored. To everyone's surprise, Flora was grinning. 'This is wild,' she said. 'What next?'

'At the bottom of the hill, the crossroads, turn right, down towards The Hope,' Tom shouted without looking over his shoulder. Within a few minutes they came to the crossroads and, weaving round several deep snowdrifts, they turned right in the direction of The Hope. The lane ran downhill into a steep-sided valley. For a time there was open ground on either side, but soon the lane dipped in between thick, wooded slopes. The trees crowded onto the verge to shut out the starry night.

'Stay together,' called Tom.

'Don't worry,' joked Flora.

The horses quickened their pace. The hair on the backs of everyone's necks began to tingle as they plunged into the darkness. Under the trees there was no snow. The hooves rang out on the road, the sharp noise piercing the stillness of the woods. They all felt as if a thousand eyes were watching them.

In a tight group they burst from the treeline, relieved to see the stars once more and glad of the silence from the snow-covered road. Tom kept up the pace until they came to the crossroads with the Peaton road. For a moment he kept them hovering in the shadow of the high hedges. The road was clear and on his signal they crossed, taking the Stanton Lacy lane in front of them.

'Just up here, we turn left onto a footpath to miss out Stanton Lacy and then we cut across the fields to Ludlow racecourse.' There was no response to Tom's instructions as everyone concentrated on staying together. Once off the road, the footpath ran alongside an open ditch and was straight and clear. As they moved off, Stanton Lacy church clock struck midnight, the chimes echoing across the wintry landscape.

Tom pushed Rakalackey into a canter and the other horses followed suit without any encouragement from their riders. They crossed the River Corve by a footbridge, forked right and came up in a rush to the white rails that marked the racecourse. The horses stood by the rails, tossing their heads and steaming in the cold night.

'Why not take the racetrack and we could go over the jumps as well?' suggested Henry.

'Don't be so stupid,' snapped Flora.

'I was only joking.' Henry laughed.

'We'll take a shortcut across the golf course.' Tom found a gap in the rails and they walked onto the course. The smooth turf was easy going and in no time they reached the minor road that bisects the golf course to join the main Ludlow to Shrewsbury road. Here too the road crosses the railway line.

'Be very careful,' called Tom. 'There is bound to be some traffic on the main road. We go straight over and onto another footpath the other side. I think we just go for it and hope for the best.' The five of them bunched up and Tom led the way over the railway bridge. Despite the hour, the main road was busy with cars and some heavy lorries.

'Pull in to the left here,' shouted Henry after a juggernaut thundered past. Tom led them over to a rough parking area on the side of the road to stand in the protection of a large ash tree. 'Wait until there are no headlights and then we all cross. Yes, Tom?' checked Henry.

'Yup, fine,' acknowledged Tom. 'There's a car coming. It's going to turn right by us. Keep still.'

The car slowed as if it was going to turn off the main road and then head across the golf course, but instead of following the road, it bumped onto the parking area. The engine cut, but blue flashing lights started to swirl on the car's roof.

'It's a police car,' squealed Flora.

Both doors opened and two policemen got out in high-visibility jackets. They shone their torches over the five riders. 'What are you lot doing at this time of night?' one of the policemen asked as they walked over to the horses.

Under his breath Tom ordered, 'When I go, we all go… OK?'

Both policemen were nearly within reach of Rakalackey when Tom kicked hard and shouted, 'Let's go.'

All the horses bolted, scattering the policemen, and followed Tom and Rakalackey over the road. From the direction of Ludlow another juggernaut could be seen bearing down on them. It was too late to turn back. The lorry slammed on its brakes, sending up smoke and the smell of burnt rubber. But they all kept their cool, reaching the safety of the other verge as the lorry let out a blast of its horn.

'That was really close,' cried Lexi, 'and what are we going to do about the police?'

'Just keep going,' shouted Tom.

Passing through a gateway, they galloped down a well-worn path that ran down the side of a plantation of young larch, but it was narrow and the horses had to stay in single file. The path led across the water meadows by the River Teme on their right. Over to their left was the main road. To everyone's dismay the police car had caught up and was now level with them, its blue light flashing and its siren wailing.

Pulling ahead, the police car suddenly stopped and both policemen jumped out. One had a loud hailer and called through a gap in the hedge, 'Stop, all of you. I repeat, stop. Return to the road immediately.'

'Not on your life,' retorted Tom, loud enough for just the others to hear. 'But it is time for a change of direction.' Tom swung Rakalackey off the path to the right and across the meadows towards the river. Off the path they fanned out, riding knee to knee, the horses relishing the soft going and freedom to stretch their legs. The policemen were left far behind, shouting through the hedge.

The river loomed up, its silver and black surface

glinting as it meandered through the fields. Clumps of elder were etched against the night sky and dark patches of reeds packed the banks to mask, in places, the river's course. 'We aren't going to wade through the river, are we?' asked Flora anxiously. 'I hate doing that.'

'Don't worry, it is shallow, the cows come down to drink here. The bank isn't steep and we'll be over in no time. Just follow me.' Tom's confidence settled any doubts.

Rakalackey and Parlour Game led the way, splashing into the water. Both horses paused to drink and then were pushed on to the far bank. Lexi and Will were right behind them. For a moment Henry hung back on Jakari, watching up and down the river and casting a backward glance.

The police car had gone and the river was still.

Chapter 20

Henry didn't see or hear the goblins until it was too late. They were marsh goblins whose natural habitat was the wetlands of far northern lands. Their horrible skill was to ambush travellers as they forded or boated river crossings. Expertly camouflaged, they were half submerged in the reed beds, their thick, leathery skin impervious to the cold water.

Lexi and Will were midstream when they struck.

Two goblins rose out of the water and swung, over their heads, ropes weighted at each end with lead balls. Let loose, the ropes flew through the air with a deadly whirring noise, to coil round the victim's arms or legs. Once their target was immobilised, the goblins were close behind with their vile curved knives.

Henry was stunned but only for a second. Instinctively, he reached for his sword under his cloak and, screaming, 'Goblins!', plunged Jakari into the river.

Will ducked at the sound of the rope beating through the air. The lethal weapon sailed over his head, landing upstream and disappearing harmlessly in the black, swirling waters. But Lexi wasn't so lucky. The rope caught her round her arms, pinning them to her side. Unable to control Lord Moose, she lost her balance and toppled from the saddle into the water.

Henry had seen Lexi fall and disappear underwater. As he urged Jakari into the middle of the river, there was no sign of her resurfacing. But the two marsh goblins were at the spot that she had fallen, their knives poised.

Leaping from Jakari's saddle, Henry's full weight landed on top of the goblins. He tried to get a grip on their bodies, but they were as slippery as eels. Henry knew they weren't the only goblins. They were bound to have reinforcements. As he groped blindly in the cold water he found Lexi's writhing body as she fought for air. In one swift movement he lifted her up and, with his dagger, cut through the rope binding her. As the sword made the cut, he pushed her away, crying out, 'Swim!'

'Do something, Tom!' screeched Flora from the far bank as Parlour Game twisted and turned in terror.

Tom jumped into the water, landing by Henry, and with their combined strength they pinned down the squirming goblins. As they fought, more wet and clammy hands wrapped themselves round their throats.

'Where's Will?' gasped Tom as he struggled with a goblin, waving a vicious-looking knife.

'Right here,' came the immediate answer. Will had swum underwater and surfaced next to Tom without warning. The goblins were caught off guard and Will's grinning face streaming water momentarily threw them into disarray. Taking advantage of this, Will grabbed two goblins and crashed their heads together with a sickening thud. He held a third goblin by its hair long enough for Henry to land a heavy punch that sent it sprawling senseless.

Over the meadows from the direction of Ludlow came the sound of two or even three sirens.

The remaining goblin hadn't expected a fight back and the unfamiliar sound of the sirens caused it added uncertainty. Will felt they had won the upper hand. 'Head for Flora,' he shouted. Flora was jumping up and down on the bank with one hand extended to them and the other holding Parlour Game. Somehow she had also gathered up Misty, but there was no sign of the other horses.

The three started wading towards the far bank. Splashing knee-deep in water, they were in reach of Flora when each one of them felt hands, like iron vices, grip their ankles underwater. They fell headlong and momentarily disappeared beneath the surface. Three more marsh goblins surfaced from the river bottom. Like lightning they sat on their victims, pushing and holding their heads underwater. Then, as the fight was beginning to ebb back in the goblins' favour, Lexi hit back.

Lexi had swum to the safety of a patch of reeds upstream, where she recovered her breath and climbed out of the water onto the riverbank. As luck would have it the three other horses, Rakalackey, Lord Moose and Jakari, were grazing close to her. They looked up as she approached but didn't shy away when she took hold of Lord Moose's reins. Then the other two were easily caught as well.

Running in a half-crouch, she led all three horses, behind a group of alder trees, back towards the crossing place. Getting closer, she could hear and then see the fight going on in midstream and realised she needed to do something quickly. Taking a firm grip of all the reins, she started down the bank, pulling the horses with her. With wild cries directed at the horses and the goblins, Lexi ran full tilt into the river.

The sight and sound of the horses plunging into the river and Lexi's mad screams made the goblins spin round to see the cause of all the commotion. They stared in disbelief, letting go of their intended victims. Sensing that they were going to be outnumbered, they half-swam and half-scrambled back to the safety of the reed beds from which they had first emerged.

'Quick, hurry,' shouted Lexi at Will, who was pulling up Tom and Henry, both exhausted and bedraggled from their brawl. 'Grab your horses.'

One of the goblins wasn't going to give up that

easily. Surging out of the reeds again, he swung his dagger at Henry's back as he was taking hold of Jakari. But Lexi had seen the danger. She shouted a warning and flung herself on the goblin as it made to bury the knife in Henry's back.

Lexi's flying tackle bowled the goblin over. Henry whirled round, startled by the crash of water behind him. The goblin surfaced and tried to stand up, still brandishing his knife. Will didn't wait to give him a second chance. He thrust his sword deep into the body of the struggling creature.

Lexi didn't allow anybody to stop and think. 'Your horses, come on.' She gulped. 'Please, let's get out of here!'

Scrambling onto the far bank, they were reunited with each of their horses. After a few false starts, everyone got back into the saddle.

'You must all be freezing?' asked Flora, who was the only one that hadn't gone into the river.

'It could be worse,' answered Lexi through chattering teeth, 'but you're right, I'm frozen.'

Tom was blue with cold as well. His teeth were chattering like mad, but he tried hard to sound cheerful, 'We've got to cross Oakley Park and then we're into Mortimer Forest.' He looked at everyone's blank faces. 'I think there are some farm buildings up here. If we can find a barn or something we can try and dry off…' Nobody answered. They broke into a stiff canter across the parkland until they reached a well-used farm track. As they joined the track they became aware for the first time of the dark silhouette on the skyline that was the edge of Mortimer Forest.

'It really isn't far now,' called Tom from the front.

As Tom had hoped, a short distance up the track was a group of farm buildings known as Hill Halton. There was a large stone-built tithe barn with a walled yard in front. As they drew close, they could hear the rustle and intermittent coughing of cattle. Tom slid off Rakalackey and opened the gate leading into the yard, and the others followed. The young heifers danced about with excitement. The warmth of the cattle mixed with the sweet smell of silage had a comforting effect on everyone's spirits.

'Can you hold my reins?' Tom asked Will. 'I will have a quick look around.'

After a couple of minutes, Tom reappeared. 'We haven't got much time, but there is a hay barn on the end. We could rub down with hay and wring our cloaks out. It's better than nothing?'

Flora giggled and everyone else laughed.

'That will do me.' Henry jumped from Jakari. 'I must do something to stop shivering.'

They took it in turns to wring out their sopping-wet clothes and rub down with hay. Flora gave Lexi her woollen jumper, telling her that her coat was more than enough to keep her warm.

'I didn't think that would make a difference,' said Will as he reappeared and took Misty's reins back from

Henry, 'but I am a lot warmer.'

As they left, Henry was the last through the yard gate and he banged it shut behind him, sending the heifers into another fit of activity. Lexi was just in front of him and hung back until he had caught up with her.

'Lexi.' Henry came up alongside her. 'Thank you for… thanks for…' Henry suddenly felt a sense of foreboding. The whole drama from start to finish flooded over him and all of a sudden he felt lost.

'You would do the same for me,' said Lexi gently.

'I know, yes, you're right. But I want this to all finish. Everything back to normal. And then I feel just the opposite. I want this to go on and on.' Henry couldn't find the right words, but as he looked at Lexi, he had an inexplicable attack of butterflies.

They rode on in silence until they caught up with the others.

*

About ten minutes after leaving Hill Halton, they crossed a quiet lane, and by Lower Whitcliffe they climbed a steep pathway that came to Mortimer Forest. As they reached the top, it was a short walk down to the Wigmore road.

'You know where to go, Henry. Take the lead.' Tom dropped back and took up Henry's position at the rear. They crossed the road and walked down to the picnic area, the table and chairs standing out in the night like patches of giant mushrooms.

Seeing the picnic area again gave Henry the feeling that he was completing a circle. Through his mind flashed his first glimpse of Gwydden, his meeting with Min and the extraordinary village in the trees, the visit to the grave of King Cleddau and the wolves that tried to stop him on his return journey.

Henry had no trouble finding the way. Under the stars the forest track shone like a white ribbon cutting through the tightly packed conifers. Jakari wanted to trot and Henry let him have his way. The rest followed suit, everyone keen to get on. Henry was watching for the place where the mountain bike track joined the main track. Recognising the landmarks, he slowed down and then with relief spotted some tyre marks that indicated where the track disappeared into the forest.

'Dismount, we walk from here,' Henry called softly.

Inside the trees it was nearly black. It took several minutes for their eyes to adjust. Even then there were regular mutterings as they stumbled and tripped their way up the path. Henry was worried about finding the place where he fell from his bike and tumbled over the edge into the hidden ravine. He had several false starts before he nearly did the same thing again. Luckily, he had a tight hold on Jakari's bridle and managed to steady himself before he went over the edge.

'It's here,' he whispered excitedly. Searching along

the top he soon found a place down. They led the horses between small outcrops of rock, where the soil was loose. By tracking diagonally down across the slope, they cautiously took sliding steps to the bottom of the ravine. Henry waited until he could see Tom was safely at the bottom, on the path, with everybody else.

'Is this it?' Flora could hardly contain herself.

'Just up here, keep together.' Henry's voice was full of anticipation too.

In single file they walked up the well-trodden path to the band of trees that hung in front of them like a curtain.

'Will,' called Henry, 'come up here, walk through with me.'

Will led Misty to stand next to Henry and together they passed through the belt of trees. Close on their heels, the others followed until they all came to stand still on the other side.

Imperceptibly the night was shifting away, the time between the last shrouds of darkness and the first inkling of dawn. A light wind was blowing a thin covering of snow and despite the flat pearl grey light, they all felt, like Henry had in the summer, entranced by the broad open valley stretching away in front of them.

The horses, restless and hungry, tried to pull at the snowy grass and on the wind came the faint sound of bells.

'Look, over there, in the distance, on the path. Somebody is coming.' Flora's sharp eyes had picked out a figure walking up the track towards them. Surrounding the lone person was the herd of goats, the billy goat proudly walking out in front.

'That,' said Henry as he stepped out down the track towards the figure, 'can only be Min.'

'Min. Is that really him?' asked Flora, running to catch up with Henry.

'Welcome back,' Min shouted, his voice full of pleasure at seeing Henry again. As he got closer Henry could see he was wearing the same green clothes. But this time, over his long fair hair, like Prince Cadell, he wore a thin gold crown. 'I cannot believe it, you really have done it!' Min reached out, putting his arm round Henry. The goats surrounded them, pushing with their noses as if they too were pleased to see visitors again.

'I've heard all about you,' said Min, smiling at Flora, who gave a little bob as if to curtsey. Min, with his arms round Henry and Flora, walked up to the others waiting with the horses.

Then at last Min came face to face with Will. The two said nothing for what seemed an age. Then Min bowed generously. 'My name is Owain, I am Prince of Gwydden, son of Gruffydd, protector of your elfish kingdom.'

'Then who am I?' asked Will.

'You are the rightful heir to the most ancient crown, a land steeped in legend, riches and beauty. A land so desperate to have a king that will lead its people out of the darkness and back to a life free of war and bloodshed, the freedom to live the elfish way of life,' said Min, looking Will straight in the eye.

'How do I believe that?'

'Look for yourself,' answered Min quietly.

Min turned to face down the valley. As far as the eye could see, small fires were being lit across the white landscape. By the light of the creeping dawn, long shadows became lines of soldiers. And as their eyes searched further afield, there were countless more armed men, rank upon rank of elfish soldiers from every corner of Gwydden. Many were fully dressed in battle order, clad in shiny breastplates, carrying shields and flags with long swallowtails that floated above them in the cold breeze. There were squadrons of elfish cavalry with their lances held high. And men and boys in their working clothes were there too. Anxious not to miss out on the extraordinary event, they had come with rough swords or pikes to show their loyalty.

As a splash of pink spread over the sky to the east, above the snow-crusted treeline, Min lifted his arms to the army gathered in the valley.

And with a shout that echoed through the valley he called, 'An elfish king stands on elfish soil.'

A great roar rose from the multitude of soldiers as the message spread down the lines. Men raised their helmets, banging their weapons on breastplates or shields. 'Lead us, lead us.' The words reverberated up and down the valley.

'You see—' said Min.

'And he is the only one who can hear the flute that Henry has round his neck,' butted in Flora.

'Exactly, thank you, Flora.' Min laughed. 'So… please believe it.'

'As I've said before, I don't think I have got much choice, have I?' Will was serious but couldn't stop a shy smile spreading across his face.

'What's next?' asked Henry, sighing with relief that Will wasn't going to be difficult.

'Oh, there is much to do. It's no small matter, but we will need to deal with the goblin empire of Sla's, there's the gold mines to recapture, particularly Llyn Caigeann, and then, of course,' continued Min, smiling, 'there will be a coronation to be fitted in somewhere.'

There was an awkward silence as the magnitude of what they had achieved started to sink in.

Tom broke the silence. 'I think we ought to be getting back. I'm thinking of the horses.'

'Yes,' agreed Henry, 'we must get going.'

As they turned to their horses, Lexi walked over to stand next to Min.

'Lexi…' said Henry, with an edge of concern, 'come on.'

'I'm staying here, Henry.'

'You cannot…' Henry stopped, her words sinking in.

Never once in all their adventures had he thought that Lexi would not now always be part of his life. From the first time he had seen her in the deli, their searches together for Will, finding him, rescuing Will from the police. She had saved his life twice, once in the castle and again as they had crossed the Teme on the way here.

'This is her home,' Min said sympathetically. 'She has done her job and she—'

'But, we—' blurted Henry.

'Henry,' Min put his hand up, 'you, Tom and Flora have done an extraordinary job finding Will and bringing him back to us. Your names are now legend. Up and down the country mothers will put their children to bed with stories of your exploits and round fires late into the night the elders will drink and smoke, talking of nothing else. In time, I am sure that Will shall take us back to the great nation we once were. And that is, in no small way, thanks to you.'

Tom put his hand on Henry's shoulder. 'Come on, we had better be going.'

'Before we go,' said Flora, 'I think you better have these back.' She pulled out of her pocket a bundle of tissue paper and held it out for Min. Taking it, he carefully opened the folds of paper. Lying in the middle were the two earrings.

'I never thought I'd see these again,' said Min, his eyes sparkling. 'Thank you.' He nodded. 'I'll keep them carefully and sometime in the future I will make sure they get a happy home.'

Lexi came over to Henry as he collected up Jakari and Lord Moose. 'Have a safe ride back. I won't forget you.'

'Thanks…' was all that Henry could manage.

Tom had hold of Rakalackey and Misty. 'Flora, you go in the middle with Parlour Game and Henry will come behind.'

They turned the horses round and walked up the short distance to the band of trees. Tom pushed his way through the low-hanging branches with Flora close on his heels. Henry stopped at the opening and turned to look back at the three figures standing on the track. Behind them the valley was bright with bonfires; the army was still spread across the landscape. Will lifted his hand in a salute as Henry ducked his head and led his two horses back through the trees.

*

The journey back was uneventful. Tom said that the fastest way home was the way they had come. It was a risk, he admitted, but somehow he felt the dangers had gone. Henry didn't comment. He was too lost in his own thoughts.

There was no sign of the goblins as they forded the river further upstream from the place they had nearly lost everything. And minutes later they crossed the main road without attracting the attention of the police.

A weak sun hung over the trees as they rode up the lane to the stables. 'I'm glad to see this place again,' said Tom cheerfully to the others over his shoulder.

'Don't speak too soon.' Henry was looking the other way and had seen the trainer in his car.

Tom's cheerfulness evaporated. 'Now we're for it.'

The trainer leant out of the car window, removing the cigarette from his mouth. 'Well done, you lot, glad somebody's out exercising.'

'Thanks,' shouted Flora cheekily. 'What's happened to the lads?'

'Overslept. Party last night.' The trainer pulled past them and disappeared off for his breakfast.

Even Henry couldn't help laughing as Tom and Flora collapsed in hysterics.

By the time they had fed and watered the horses and rugged them up, a few lads had appeared. One of them agreed to drop them back in Ludlow. He had to go and buy a new battery for the pick-up, he explained.

*

As Henry climbed the stairs to his room he felt totally exhausted. Opening his bedroom door, he pulled off his boots and threw himself straight onto the bed. He felt angry and dejected. Letting out his frustration, he banged his head hard into the pillow.

Lying there, he pushed his hands under the pillow, his fingers unexpectedly curling round a package. He sat up and pulled out a tiny parcel. The wrapping was the distinctive blue and white paper used by the deli to wrap cheese.

Undoing it, he found a lock of reddy-brown hair tied with a neat, green ribbon. Scrawled inside the paper was a message: 'See you later.'

Henry flopped back on his bed. He pulled the flute from around his neck, running his fingers over the ivory carving. Perhaps, after all, this wasn't the end. Perhaps it was just the beginning of the beginning.

Acknowledgments

I started writing The Tree Elves of Ludlow a number of years ago when my children still had bed time stories. Turning this story into a published book has a lot to do with Letty, my daughter-in-law. After badgering me to read the book, she told me in no uncertain terms to find a publisher. I cannot thank her enough.

I will always be grateful to The Book Guild for believing wholeheartedly in the book. I am also indebted to Margaret Wilson who agreed to edit the book. Her encouragement and skills were invaluable. To my sister Clare, a big thank you for all her diligent proof reading and intuitive comments.

I have loved working with Jenny Jones whose wonderful illustrations have bought this book alive. She is a special person as well as a hugely talented artist.

Thank you to all my children and step children who unwittingly are the heroes of this book.

And of course, Milly my wife who has never stopped having faith in me and helping to get this book over the line.